The Golden Knife

Cuchillo Oro knew there was a good chance he was going to die, but he had no intention of submitting meekly to the band of drunken Apaches advancing upon him. He was close to exhaustion from a cruel combination of hunger, thirst, and lack of sleep. But such things were merely physical—they could not subjugate the spirit of a purebred Apache brave. If he was to die, then some of those intent upon taking his life would lose their own. The golden knife for which he had been named would be dripping blood before it fell from his dead hand.

The Apache Series

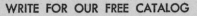

#5 FORT TREACHERY
by William M. James
Apache

PINNACLE BOOKS • NEW YORK CITY

This is a work of fiction. All the characters and events portrayed in this book are fictional, and any resemblance to real people or incidents is purely coincidental.

APACHE: FORT TREACHERY

Copyright © 1975 by William M. James

An original Pinnacle Books edition, published for the first time anywhere.

ISBN: 0-523-00782-5

Cover illustration by Larry Kresek

First printing, December 1975

Printed in the United States of America

PINNACLE BOOKS, INC.
275 Madison Avenue
New York, N.Y. 10016

for

Jane and Elizabeth—
who regularly get
dictated to!

FORT TREACHERY

CHAPTER ONE

Cuchillo Oro knew there was a good chance he was going to die, but he had no intention of submitting meekly to the band of drunken Apaches advancing upon him. He was close to exhaustion from a cruel combination of hunger, thirst, and lack of sleep. But such things were merely physical—they could not subjugate the spirit of a purebred Apache brave. If he was to die, then some of those intent upon taking his life would lose their own. The golden knife for which he had been named would be dripping blood before it fell from his dead hand.

Cuchillo was crouched in a small depression just below the ridge of a rise. He was naked except for hide leggings, moccasins, and headband. And his only weapon was the knife thrust into the waistband of his leggings. Thus, even as he crouched and watched the twenty braves draw closer to his place of concealment, the agonies of his deprivation were brutally increased. For the noon sun beat down out of the

1

cloudless sky to sear every unprotected surface. But Cuchillo did not sweat, for his secretion glands were dry. Too much moisture had been pumped and drawn from his body already. He felt as drained and arid as the earth and rock of Arizona Territory spread beneath and around him.

But no man is ever barren of water until he is dead for many days, and Cuchillo worked some saliva into his mouth. Not much, but enough to run a slightly moist tongue over his lips. He moved a little, shifting most of his weight from one folded leg to the other so that neither limb became set. And he leaned forward from the waist to widen his range of vision and keep every advancing Indian in sight.

They were moving up the slope in an uneven line, without stealth: and their reckless confidence did not come entirely from the liquor which they sucked out of stolen bottles as they staggered and weaved over the uneven ground. They knew they were stalking a single quarry and they had no reason to believe he was armed —even with the knife.

The senseless pursuit had begun an hour ago, which was half a day after Cuchillo had been forced to slit the throat of his horse. The animal, as close to exhaustion as its rider, had stumbled on the treacherous rocks of an arroyo and snapped a foreleg. That was many miles out on the desert plain to the north and the death of the horse was inevitable. Had not Cuchillo been a Mimbreños Apache—and a grandson of the great chief Mangas Coloradas—he might have sunk to the ungiving ground beside the carcass of the animal and submitted to death under the fast rising sun. But his heritage—and his chosen mission—would not allow such a thing. It was not even a conscious decision to rise and stumble on, striking out for the distant range of hills to the south. But, once on the move again, he did resume control over the plan to cheat death. Although he wavered from side to side and often tripped on the cracked and broken ground when his heavy lids dropped to blind his pained eyes, he always struggled to recover. And, when the heat shimmer closed around him to shroud the far-off hill country, he constantly checked to ensure that the sun was on his left. Later, the very cruelty of nature that had brought him so close to death offered him an incentive to continue living. A half dozen buzzards, their talons and beaks crusted with the dried blood of the horse, began to circle on the high thermals above his punished form. And—whenever he thought he had drawn upon the final reserves of his strength—he looked up at the gracefully soaring birds and discovered fresh vitality deep inside him.

Cuchillo Oro would have been a good meal for the scavenger birds, despite the weakening results of recent adversity. He was extremely tall for an Apache brave, standing at a height of six feet three inches. And still broadly built, for temporary lack of food and water did not reduce bone and muscle: only excess fat, and he had none of this. Above the high, strong body and powerful limbs was the head of a man which looked and thought as the epitome of the Apache breed. Framed by thick, jet-black hair, which fell from under the broad headband to brush his shoulders, Cuchillo had a face that was classically handsome. The eyes, as dark as a moonless night, were narrow and set deep under the high, flat brow. The nose was finely formed, narrow between the elevated cheekbones then broadening to flared nostrils. The mouth was wide above an aggressively thrusting jawline.

There was not a single natural flaw in the brave's physical appearance. But man's inhumanity to man—specifically the cruel hatred of one white man for this Indian—had left a mark upon him. A knife and then a bullet had hacked and blasted away the index and middle finger of Cuchillo's right hand. The act had been one of cold-blooded torture, its cruelty intensified by the fact that it was in punishment for a crime of which the Apache was innocent.

Because he had the mind of an Indian warrior descended from a great chief, influenced only slightly by the teachings of the lone White

Eyes he called a friend, such unwarranted punishment had been sufficient to give Cuchillo Oro his mission—to kill the man who tortured him. But his agony did not end with mere physical pain. The same White Eyes had also murdered his wife and baby son. And the unsuppressible mental anguish that this unleashed could not be appeased.

Thus it was that, after the soaring and wheeling buzzards ceased to act as a spur to the struggling Apache, a mental image of Cyrus L. Pinner forced him to keep moving toward the shimmer-shrouded hills. For if Cuchillo Oro perished, the evil cavalry captain would be allowed to live until he died by another's hand or his soul was claimed by the Great Spirit.

As the sun climbed higher and beat down more fiercely upon the weakening Indian, the heat haze—creating its wickedly tantalizing mirages of cool water lakes—closed in tighter around the staggering figure. But the hill country was in sight now! He didn't have to keep turning his heavy-lidded eyes toward the sun to get his bearings. He could see his objective. The important thing to do now was to think positively. There would certainly be shade up there in the hills. Maybe some game to stealthily hunt and kill. And, less likely but possible, a waterhole. The very thought of a means to slake his thirst rose saliva into Cuchillo's mouth and he moistened his cracked and blistering lips. But there was nothing he could do to relieve the harsh burning sensation on the firm flesh of his torso and arms. Only a long rest out of the direct heat of the sun would ease this.

He reached the lower slopes of the hill country at the northern end of the Dragoon Mountains and found little comfort there. The terrain was mostly barren rock and hard-packed dirt almost incapable of supporting vegetation. Here and there grew clumps of staghorn cholla, ocotillo, and saguaro: but never thick or high enough to give shade to a man of his stature. The incline was not steep, but to such a weakened and dehydrated frame it was like scaling an almost sheer wall.

Then he crested that first, inhospitable rise and a smile parted his pained lips and injected a glint of hope into his red-rimmed eyes. He was looking down into a shallow valley and, on the opposite slope—midway up to the jagged ridge—he could see a group of caves. Their entrances were a refreshing black against the white and gray of the bleached terrain. Because of the way the rock was fashioned, the caves faced slightly to the east: but, by the time he had covered the half-mile walking distance, the sun would have shifted and he would be able to find shelter from its harsh rays.

He seemed to command a renewed strength as he started downward, toward the floor of the valley. But he made the mistake of overestimating his capabilities. His forward momentum built up until he found himself running against his will. The downward slope carried him faster and faster and he was unable to stop. The inevitable happened and, nearing the valley floor, a leg muscle collapsed under the strain and he pitched to the ground. Every bone in his body was jarred by the impact. Then bruises were raised upon bruises as he turned head-over-heels, forced himself sideways on to the slope, and hurtled into a roll. Alone in the wilderness, out of sight and earshot of witnesses, the Apache allowed himself the luxury of grunts and groans as his body was subject to this new form of punishment.

Then the slope ran out and he came to an abrupt halt in a tangled heap of arms and legs wrapped around his aching body. Even while his mind played tricks on him, continuing to hold a moving image of sky and land spinning about one another, his hand reached the waistband of his leggings. The knife was still there.

It was no ordinary knife such as an Apache, or even a horsesoldier, might be expected to carry. It was an Italian *Cinquedea*, which had been made in the fifteenth century, with a double-edged blade of the finest steel. The contoured handle was of ivory and it had a curved hilt of solid gold inlaid with precious gems. A very valuable knife: but it was not because of its intrinsic worth that Pinner had prized it so highly. The knife had been presented to his father and Captain—then Lieutenant—Pinner had inherited the weapon. Such a reason for pride of possession Cuchillo could understand and respect.

But it was not he who had stolen the golden knife from its owner. A thieving White Eyes had done this, and had then pretended the weapon was his to trade. Pinner could have discovered this had he tried, but his hatred of Apaches was so great that he had not been prepared to look further than the young brave who he saw with the knife. Thus had the bitter feud been unleashed between the White Eyes horsesoldier and the Apache. First the brutal mutilation of the Indian's hand, then the slaughter of his wife and son. Cuchillo became Cuchillo Oro and regained possession of the knife. And, like its previous owner, the Apache was unconcerned with its financial value. Unlike Pinner, he did not have any pride in its possession. He carried it as a symbol of the evil that had been done to him: and in the hope that he would be able to use it to kill his bitter enemy.

After ensuring that the knife had not been lost during the tumble down the slope, Cuchillo tested his legs and arms. They were painfully bruised, but there were no breaks or even sprains. For a few moments he lay still, drawing in deep breaths. Then, as he started to rise, he heard voices. And he was gripped by an almost light-headed exhilaration. Although the men were far off and many were shouting at the same time, he was able to pick out the odd word: and these words were spoken in the guttural Apache tongue.

He heard: ". . . horsesoldiers. . . ." "Firewater. . . ." White Eyes squaws. . . ." "Kill. . . ." and several obscenities. He got to his feet and began to detect tones of voice in addition to disjointed words. All the men were slurring, obviously under the influence of hard liquor. Cuchillo had a taste for the whiskey of the White Eyes himself, but at this moment it was plain and simple water his parched throat and puckered stomach were demanding.

He stood looking toward the east, squinting against the sun. The Apaches were approaching from this direction, their gleeful voices filtering through a scattering of large boulders that lay across the floor of the shallow valley. He cupped his hands around his mouth and tried to shout a greeting. But only a choked, low-volume cry emerged. Acrid bile rose into his throat in the wake of the sound and if he had eaten recently he would have vomited the contents of his stomach.

Then two Indians emerged from among the boulders, leading their ponies by rope reins with one hand while they used the other to upend bottles into their mouths. The sun bounced against the bottles and lanced painful rays of dazzling light into Cuchillo's eyes. The two braves saw Cuchillo suddenly. They halted and stared at him, over a distance of four hundred yards. Too far away for Cuchillo to see their faces. But he could see the manner of their dress. Both wore wide-brimmed hats and hide leggings. One was barefoot and the other wore riding boots. One had a Cavalry sergeant's tunic draped over his bare shoulders while the other wore a store-bought shirt. Tunic and shirt were both bloodstained. Dried blood also encrusted the scalps which hung from the braves' gun belts.

"New prey!" one of them yelled, hurling aside his bottle and drawing a revolver from his holster.

"Another scalp!" the second countered. He took a renewed swig at the bottle as he hauled his gun clumsily from the holster.

Both revolvers cracked at once. One bullet kicked up a divot of dirt ten yards in front of Cuchillo. The other whined high over his head. The shouts and the shots brought a bunch of other Apaches running from the boulders. Cuchillo held his ground for a few more moments. The braves who came into sight now were similarly dressed in an assortment of Apache attire and a mixture of the clothing worn by White Eyes soldiers and civilians. Some had claimed scalps and others had not.

But all were armed with guns—two of them carrying repeater rifles. Most had bottles.

Cuchillo remained where he was in the hope that at least one of the braves was not too drunk to recognize a fellow Apache. But, when a barrage of gunfire exploded a hail of bullets toward him, he whirled and lunged into a run. One of the guns to crack out was a rifle, and its bullet whipped close enough to him to breathe a slipstream across his upper arm.

Then his own breathing and a rushing sound in his ears subdued all other noise. But there was no more shooting. He would have heard the crack of gun reports. All he did hear through the sounds of his own exertion were more disjointed words, slurred still but with a new tone of high excitement.

". . . Kill." "Indian . . ." "Apache . . ." "Quiet . . ." "Must not."

Cuchillo, cruelly snatched from the hope of deliverance and plunged into the threat of sudden death, discovered yet another reserve of strength. His long legs pumped beneath him, carrying him up the slope toward the black holes of the caves. He shot a glance over his shoulder and saw that even more Indians had appeared from amid the boulders. All were like him—Mimbreños in their early twenties—but there the similarity ended. Renegades, too, but they were banded together, roaming like a pack of animals. Perhaps they had been driven from

11

their *rancheria* by the injustices of the White Eyes.

Not that it mattered. Such things were academic, as John Hedges—Cuchillo's White Eyes teacher—would say. It was important only that a band of Mimbreños was intent upon killing a brother from the same tribe. They had already killed many White Eyes—the scalps told of this. And had stolen much whiskey to heighten the effects of their triumph. But whiskey in the belly was no substitute for the spilling of blood —even Apache blood.

Cuchillo, his strong desire for survival continuing to power strength through his body, reached the caves in the hillside. And he rejected them. They offered the promised shelter from the sun: and cover from gunfire—if a man had the means to keep his attackers at bay. If no such means were available, each cave was no more than a trap and ready-made grave.

He hesitated only for a moment to glance into the caves, and then back down the slope toward his pursuers. A brave almost as tall as Cuchillo Oro had emerged as the leader of the band. His symbol of rank was the saber of a horsesoldier that he thrust out in front of him as he headed the braves. By his order, all revolvers had been holstered. The two men with rifles had dropped out of the chase and were

12

waiting with the ponies, three of which were hitched to trevois piled high with loot.

Perhaps the braves had seen the near-exhaustion of Cuchillo. Or perhaps the drunken minds had decided upon a code of honor that would not allow mounted men to pursue a lone prey on foot. Then again, perhaps they wanted to prolong the sport.

As he lunged into another run up the slope, Cuchillo decided that the last reason was the real one. It also explained why guns had been banned. Drunk as they were, the more than a score of Indians could have killed him easily had they chased him on their ponies and exploded a barrage of gunfire at him.

The pursuers were on the rising ground now, angling away from the ponies on a diagonal sprint across the slope. They sucked from bottles as they ran, and vented high-pitched war cries as each gulp of liquor spread fire through their bellies. Some wielded knives and tomahawks, the steel blades glinting in the high, bright sunlight.

Cuchillo attained the rocky, jagged crest of the valley side and had to slow his pace to pick a way through the uneven strip. Then the ground became smooth again, dipping slightly and then rising to another crest, like the trough between two waves on a stormy ocean. Recalling the increased impetus that had sent him crashing to the ground before, Cuchillo did not allow momentum to carry him faster than he had the actual strength to go. He attained the new crest as his pursuers reached the first one. A glance back at them showed the mouths in their sweat-run faces gaped to vent further war cries. But now his breathing and the rushing in his ears blotted out every sound that did not emit from within himself.

He broke across a small plateau, half-stumbled and recovered before he pitched to the ground. He swung to the west and a glimmer of hope sprang up inside his pounding head. Liquor was a treacherous intoxicant. While seeming to slake a man's thirst it did, in large quantities, dehydrate him. If they continued to suck from the bottles as they ran, the Apaches at his back might quickly become as exhausted as he was.

But then he knew that such a hope was as self-deceiving as the liquor. His pursuers were fresh, and they were exhilarated from a recent triumph over the White Eyes. Cuchillo was close to being a broken man. He had traveled far north from his border homeland on the strength of a rumor that the hated Captain Pinner had been given command of an isolated army post on the Rio Puerco. There had been truth to the rumor, but the assignment had been a temporary one. Pinner had left and gone south again before Cuchillo reached the post. Frustration had hung heavy within the Apache as he had turned his pony to retrace his trail back toward the Sonora border.

Short of supplies, he had sought help from a small *rancheria* near the Mescaleros. But they'd had little enough for themselves. Nothing to give away: but food and water to trade with. And, faced with the vast stretch of barren desert between himself and his enemy, Cuchillo had been forced to trade. All his clothing except for the leggings and moccasins, plus his fully loaded Spencer rifle, in exchange for a pitiful quantity of the necessities of life on the desert.

He was cheated and knew it but there had been nothing to do except accept the situation. Several young braves among the Mescaleros had sensed his resentment and his own rifle was among the weapons which threatened him as he was forced to leave the *rancheria*. The supplies had been exhausted a day and a half ago. He had been walking half a day.

To hope he could reduce his pursuers to a greater degree of weakness than himself was a sign that his mind was beginning to reach the same state of exhaustion as his body.

At the far side of the plateau there was a steep, fifty foot drop into a narrow gorge. He had to scramble down it backward, feet and hands hooking into niches and over tiny ledges. This represented a more substantial hope of escape. His pursuers would be unable to make the climb in a close-knit group. If he could reach the bottom of the gorge and find a hiding place, perhaps one or two of the drunken Apaches would get down before the others. If he could finish such front runners with the knife and get at least one gun. . . .

"Keep running, my brother!" a voice taunted from above him. "As an Apache, you should not die as easily as this."

Cuchillo glanced down, saw he had only six feet to go, and released his hand grips as he kicked out with his feet. He landed, evenly balanced, and glanced up the side of the gorge. A dozen grinning faces looked down at him. Then a barrage of empty whiskey bottles were hurled in his direction. Even though he whirled quickly and lunged into a new run, two of the bottles struck him painfully on the back and shoulders. The gorge swung into a curve and Cuchillo shot a glance over his shoulder before he plunged out of sight. Four braves were already scrambling down the near-sheer rock face and another three were close above them. Another hope was dashed. He rounded the curve and the gorge broadened into an area of low mounds rolling toward a long incline a half-mile distant.

Without breaking his stride, Cuchillo ran up and over each mound in turn. In his mind was the strong fear that if he stopped he would crumple to the ground and be unable to raise himself. He reached the higher hill and lumbered up this. At no time did he look back for he had a second fear—of losing his balance, which would have the same result as stopping. His breathing was louder and more ragged than ever. The sound filling his ears was like that of water gushing over a cataract. He saw the shallow depression just below the crest of the hill and he half-leaped, half-fell into it. He lay on his back, gasping for air, for a full minute. Then, drawing the knife, he rolled over on to his belly and crawled up to the lip of the hole. Through a natural barricade of rocks perched on the rim, he blinked out across an empty landscape.

For long moments of near delirium, Cuchillo thought he had daydreamed the images of the drunken pursuers. But reason prevailed and he knew they were real. A half minute passed and he saw one of his tormentors. It was the brave with the sabre, and he was mounted—galloping a pony out of the mouth of the gorge. Then animal and rider disappeared again, behind one of the low rises. Two minutes were sliced from time and everything remained silent and unmoving. Cuchillo's heart ceased to race and his breathing rate slowed. The rushing sound faded from his ears. A pain started in his chest. The sun beat down upon him and seemed to burn holes into his naked back and shoulders. An ache began to throb in his head.

Then he saw the entire group of Apaches

again. They appeared on the brow of the previously concealing mound, spread out in a line with the now unmounted leader at the center. Every brave had a fresh bottle.

"Apache!" the group's chief bellowed. "I know you can hear me! I saw back there!" He pointed with the sabre toward the mouth of the gorge. "You are weary with travel and the chase! You are close to here because your strength has failed you! We, too, are weary. But we have refreshed ourselves!" He upended the bottle to his lips and sucked a great swig from it. "The fire-water gives us new heart! Now we come to cut out your heart!"

He started forward and his followers matched his progress, spreading out to lengthen the line and thus cover every square inch of terrain between themselves and Cuchillo Oro. The prey inched forward as the hunters started up the incline, pressing his face between two rocks to keep the entire line of Indians in sight. The sun reached its noon day peak and began its slow decline toward the west. But many hours would pass before it lost any of its intense heat. The hunters were so close now he could hear the gurgling sounds made by the hard liquor as it was tipped down their throats. His own throat felt more arid than ever by contrast.

Cuchillo prepared to die. He curled himself up into a ball. But he was not cowering. The two Apaches directly in line with his hiding place were only ten staggering paces away. The advance was a zig-zag, with some Indians fallen back and others several yards ahead. Cuchillo was both curled and coiled: curled to stay in the cover of the rocks for the longest possible time, and coiled to lunge into killing movement when time ran out.

The knife would thrust at least once. If it could be twice—and fast enough—there was even a chance he could capture two revolvers. And if the bodies fell into the dip and they carried spare ammunition . . . He chided himself against the futility of dreaming ahead of the reality.

"Horsesoldiers!" a brave cried. His fear sounded through the slurred tone of the single word.

The two braves advancing on Cuchillo's position came to an abrupt halt. The same brand of fear that had sounded in the voice showed on their faces. They, and Cuchillo, glanced to either side, looking along the straggled line of braves. Every hunter had halted. Then all eyes swept fearful gazes up the slope toward a brave who was crouched at the crest.

"I count at least one hundred!" the brave reported, turning from looking over the hill crest to stare at his startled companions.

"Stay where you are!" the chief ordered, and

lowered into a crouch to scuttle up toward the crest.

Cuchillo risked interrupting his watch on the nearest Apaches to look in the same direction as they were. The crouching brave and chief were fifty yards to the right of the concealing depression, their postures rigid as they peered over at what lay beyond the rise. Then, after a few moments, they withdrew far enough down the slope to stand erect without danger of being skylined.

"He speaks right!" the chief announced. "Many horsesoldiers. Maybe as many as he says. One mile distant. We go."

The chief was obeyed without a single word being spoken. The braves remained where they were until he had moved behind the line. Then they followed him, closing in to form a tight-knit group. There was no more drinking, but neither did any brave discard his bottle. Cuchillo eased out of his curled position and small bones in his limbs cracked as they were released from tension. The departing Apaches, moving faster now than they had in advance, went from sight and reappeared by turns as they hurried across the undulating terrain. When they emerged from behind the last mound, angling toward the mouth of the gorge, the chief was astride his pony.

Cuchillo rolled over on to his back to protect the burned flesh from further assault by the fierce sun. He closed his eyes against the glare and curled back his blistered lips to bare his teeth in an expression that was half grimace-half grin.

"Cuchillo give whole lot of thanks for help from unexpected quarter," he croaked.

CHAPTER TWO

Cuchillo's punished back was suffering in the direct heat of the sun again, for he was stretched out on his belly at the crest of the hill. His vantage point was the same as that used by the chief and the brave and he gazed down on the same scene they had witnessed.

A hundred horsesoldiers was about the right number. They were formed into a column riding in ranks of two with a supplies wagon at the rear. They were closer than a mile away now, riding their mounts at an easy walk along the floor of a broad valley. The high ground from which Cuchillo looked down formed one side of the valley which cut east to west through the hill country. Bare rock all the way to the bottom, then a dust-covered floor. The hooves of the horses kicked up dust that shrouded the column like a long streak of early-morning mist.

Rested, albeit for a short time, Cuchillo was able to see more clearly now. Familiar with the symbols of rank worn by the army—from the days when he had lived on the borderline *rancheria* close to Fort Davidson—he saw that the column was led by a lieutenant. It was odd that such a large body of men should be under the command of such a junior officer. But a clue to the reason for this was that several of the cavalrymen had been recently wounded: they wore bandages on limbs and heads, in some cases the dust-grayed whiteness of the dressings spotted or patched by seeping blood. And, hitched to the rear of the supplies wagon were half a dozen saddled and riderless horses. The soldiers had obviously been engaged in a fight and perhaps had lost their senior commander.

As the head of the column drew level with Cuchillo's position, the lieutenant spoke to a sergeant riding immediately behind him and the noncom raised a hand to halt the men. The long cloud of dust settled and the lieutenant raised to his eyes the binoculars that hung around his neck. Cuchillo ducked out of sight as the glasses swept over the crest of the hill where he was watching. He heard shouts and, when he looked down into the valley again, he saw a man break from the column at the rear and canter his horse up to rein it to a halt beside the officer. The man wore a forage cap and army tunic bearing corporal's chevrons. But his pants were of hide and there were moccasins on his feet. He was an Indian.

He listened intently to the instructions he

23

was given, and acknowledged them with a sloppy salute. Then he heeled his horse into a gallop, heading diagonally across the slope towards a point several hundred yards to the west of where Cuchillo watched.

A plan was hurriedly formulated in Cuchillo's mind and he pushed himself backward, away from the hill crest, until he was able to rise to his full height. Then he made a further demand upon his diminished strength, and lunged into yet another sprint. But this time there was a difference. Instead of being the hunted, he had become the hunter. The switch of roles did a great deal to push back the limit of his endurance.

He could guess the instructions which had been given the Indian scout. At the point on the hill crest to which he was riding—and Cuchillo was running—there was a stumpy outcrop of rock. A million years of weather had carved numerous niches into the sandstone. A man could climb the thirty foot high tower easily: and from the top would have a fine vantage point to survey the surrounding country.

Cuchillo knew he could never have outrun the mounted scout on level ground over the same distance. But the scout was galloping up a slope and had three times the distance to cover as Cuchillo. The Indian on foot reached the outcrop ahead of the Indian astride the horse. He went to the far side of the sandstone,

24

gasping to regain his breath as he sagged against the sun-warmed rock, and listened to the hoofbeats of the horse. As the Indian spoke to the animal—in a tongue foreign to the waiting Apache—Cuchillo drew the golden knife. The horse halted and the Indian slid from the saddle. As he hobbled the animal, he continued to speak to it and Cuchillo recognized the occasional word. It was Yuman. He chanced a glance around the rock and decided the stockily built, middle-aged Indian was a Mohave.

Cuchillo, in such a desperate situation, would have killed a fellow Apache without compunction. But he knew his future sleep would be less troubled since his victim was not of his tribe. The Mohave turned from hobbling his horse to glance up at the easy climb. He raised a hand to wave, showing that he was still in sight of the soldiers below, then shuffled to the side to commence the ascent at the base of the easiest route.

He was a good scout. As he hooked his hands into the first holds, he sensed the presence of another man. But he was not skilled in the art of the fast draw. He wore a regulation army gun belt with a Frontier Colt jutting from the unbuttoned holster. He became rigid as he sensed the nearness of Cuchillo. Then, using one of his hands to power himself, he whirled. The other hand dropped from the rock to drape the butt of the Colt.

Cuchillo had stepped from hiding the instant he was aware the Mohave had poised for a move. The knife was held above his shoulder, the gap between the two Indians dictating a throw rather than a thrust. A sweat of fear beaded the lined and puckered face of the Mohave. The knife spun through the air, sun glinting on the blade and dancing on the jeweled hilt. The gun was only half out of the holster when the needle-sharp point of the blade pierced tunic and shirt to find flesh. Cuchillo hurled himself in the wake of the ornate weapon, hands stretched out in front of him to the limit of his arm reach.

The gun cleared the holster. The knife penetrated deep into the Mohave's chest, cutting through tissue between two bones of the rib cage to find the heart. The dying man gaped his mouth wide to scream. A reflex to pain caused his finger to squeeze the trigger as his thumb slipped off the cocked hammer. Cuchillo was in mid-air, almost horizontal to the ground, when his hands found their target. One clamped over the wide mouth of the Mohave, silencing the scream before it could clear the throat. One of the good two fingers of his mutilated right hand hooked between the hammer and firing pin of the Colt. The remaining fingers of the hand clawed around the revolver and fastened a tight grip as both men collapsed to the ground, the dead one protecting the live one from the full force of impact. The only sounds of the killing were the thud of the knife burying itself to the hilt in flesh, Cuchillo's sharp intake of breath and the thud of the men against the ground. The sole witness was the scout's gelding, which looked at the scene with a disinterested eye.

"My apologies, Indian," the Apache muttered as he raised into a crouch beside the corpse of the Mohave. "But, as Cuchillo says, sometimes men must die so that others may live."

He knew that the horsesoldiers would be staring up the slope toward the outcrop, watching for their scout to climb into view: and that, when there was no sign of him, a party would be sent to investigate. Cuchillo had some grisly work to do before this happened.

He withdrew the knife from the wound and it came free with a subdued sucking sound. Because the Mohave had been dead for several seconds, there was just a small spurt of blood. But soon, as Cuchillo slashed, cut, and sliced with the knife, the dry ground upon which the body lay became spattered and ran with bright crimson. First he scalped the scout. Then he stabbed out the eyes, sliced off the nose, and slit the tongue in two.

Working with a look of tense concentration on his handsome face, he ripped the clothes from the chest of the dead man and marked the flesh with a dozen slashing cuts. Finally, he cut away the pants at the crotch and castrated the unfeeling corpse.

"Again, my apologies," the Apache said softly, and there was a look of genuine concern and compassion in his dark eyes. "But to die quickly is better than to live slowly. I know this thing."

He had been careful not to allow the spilled blood to stain his flesh and sparse clothing. Now he wiped the knife scrupulously clean on the torn shirt of the dead Indian. From below, he could hear shouts, too far off for the words to be discerned. But the beat of galloping hooves was unmistakable. He glanced quickly around him, beyond the ground on which the blood was already crusting and changing color from crimson to black. The hard rock showed no footprints. He allowed himself a single self-torturing look at the canteen hung from the saddlehorn on the back of the bored gelding. But to steal from the man he had killed might spoil his plan.

He whirled and ran—down the slope and away from the sound of the rapidly approaching horsemen. He reached the foot of the decline, raced up the first low rise, and threw himself full-length to the ground on the other side. He heard shouts of surprise and horror cutting across the sounds of horses being skidded to a halt. He inserted the knife up his leggings from his ankles and tightened two of the encircling thongs to hold it securely in place. Then he crawled up to the crest of the mound and peered across at the base of the outcrop.

A sergeant and a corporal had dismounted to examine the mutilated body of the Mohave. Four enlisted men were still in their saddles, eyes and rifles raking the undulating terrain.

"Lieutenant!" the sergeant yelled, hands cupped around his mouth as he swung away from the body and strode to the side of the rock tower to look down into the valley. "Hunter Man's dead and butchered and—"

"Sarge!" one of the enlisted men cut in, and squeezed the trigger of his Spencer.

Cuchillo had purposely showed himself, starting to rise from the cover of the hill as he thrust his hands high into the air. The bullet cracked close to him, between his head and upraised right arm. "They're comin'!"

The Apache threw himself back to the ground as all six men swung toward him. The other three soldiers still in the saddle joined the other one in leaping from their horses, snapping off a fusillade of shots as they did so. Splinters of rock exploded from the crest of the rise showered down upon Cuchillo.

"Friend!" he yelled, but his voice was still as weak as his body, and a second volley en-

29

sured there was no chance of his shout being heard.

Further away than where the six soldiers were sprawled on the ground beside the outcrop, other shouts were raised. But the patrol were too concerned with checking the terrain for signs of other Indians to spend time calling out answers. Cuchillo was less trusting this time. He raised just a hand above the cover of the rise. He waved it.

"There, sarge!" a man called, half-excited, half-afraid.

"Hold your fire!" the noncom barked. Then he raised his voice to a bellow. "Injun, you talk English?"

Cuchillo tried to get some saliva into his mouth, hopeful it would add power to his voice. But the act produced merely a dry retching sound from deep in his throat. "I speak it good!" he answered. The words were no more than croaking whispers.

"Answer me, you bastard Injun!" the sergeant bellowed.

Cuchillo's arm was still raised and in sight. He knew he had to risk showing himself in total again. First he put up the other arm, then he went up into a crouch. The six soldiers lay in the prone position, Spencer rifles zeroed in on him. He straightened to his full height, then stepped up on to the crest of the rise.

"Hot damn, they're surrenderin'!" a man exclaimed.

The distance between the Apache and the soldiers was about two hundred and fifty yards. But the hot, still air was so silent the voices carried easily.

"One of 'em's surrenderin'!" the noncom corrected in a growling tone. "And that could mean there's a whole friggin' bunch of others gettin' ready to jump us." He raised his voice again. "I asked you a question, Injun."

"I speak!" Cuchillo called.

"He's talkin' sergeant," the corporal reported. "But he ain't talkin' very loud."

One of the enlisted men spat. "I reckon he'll yell real loud iffen I plug a bullet in his guts."

"Shuddup!" the sergeant snarled, and eased upright, never allowing his rifle to waver in its aim toward Cuchillo. "Anyone blasts the bastard, it'll be me!" Then, to Cuchillo. "If you understand what I'm sayin', Injun, start walkin' over this way."

The Apache moved and the walk was the hardest traveling he had had to do since after he slit the throat of his horse out on the broiling desert. The six aimed rifles meant he was at his closest to death. And, after he had covered just a few yards, the strain of holding his arms high above his head reached an almost unbearable proportion. He admitted to himself that he had completed his final act of survival

31

on this day. His last reserve of energy was dripping out of him with every step he took and no matter what kind of threat was directed at him now, he would be unable to combat it by even the mildest form of retaliation.

As he started up the slope toward where all six soldiers were now standing erect, his vision blurred and did not clear. It took as much effort to keep his arms high as to drag one foot in front of the other.

"Hurry it up, you murderin' skunk of an Injun!" somebody snarled at him.

"Shuddup!" the just recognizable voice of the sergeant retorted. "This guy is about done in."

"So finish him, sarge."

There was a background noise to the voices. It took Cuchillo's fuzzed mind several seconds to work out what it was. The thunder of many hooves as horses were spurred into a full gallop. He reached the lip of the slope where the ground leveled out at the base of the sandstone outcrop. Reflected sun glared off the buttons of the soldiers' uniforms and added darkness to the blurring of Cuchillo's vision.

"Hold it right there, Injun!" the sergeant barked.

Cuchillo was four feet from where the soldiers stood. He brought one foot alongside the other and fought against the swaying motion that was trying to unbalance him. The sergeant was the one doing all the talking and Cuchillo concentrated his blurred gaze on the noncom. He was a short man with a bulging stomach and a very red face out of which his eyes stared with bitter hatred. He sloped the rifle to his shoulder as he stepped up close to the Apache, who was a foot taller. Cuchillo guessed the man's age was about fifty. He was looking into the face, expecting a question or order to be barked at him. But the sergeant's free hand, bunched into a fist, slammed against Cuchillo's stomach.

The blow was the final assault: all that was necessary to break the cruelly punished Indian. Pride and spirit collapsed and the physical body of the Apache followed. Air whooshed out of his lungs as he folded forward, then sat down hard. His arms dropped to his sides and his hands clawed at the source of the agony.

"I ain't no lover of Injuns," the sergeant announced unnecessarily, shouting to be heard above the swelling sound of hoofbeats. "Apaches I hate worst of all."

He tipped the Spencer forward, catching the barrel in his free hand and angling it down at the helpless Cuchillo. He bent his body at the waist, giving himself the extra inches to ease the muzzle of the rifle under Cuchillo's jaw. He applied pressure to force up the head so that the two men could lock stares.

"Give me one reason I shouldn't kill you?" he demanded.

The pain in his stomach was the most severe of all Cuchillo's agonies now, but he forced his lean features to adopt the lines of a neutral expression. His voice croaked the response, as the other five soldiers crowded in closer to hear the words. "I can lead you to Indians who killed your scout."

Many men—perhaps half those who had formed the column in the barren valley—rode into sight along the hill crest. Rifles were out of the boots and the lieutenant had his revolver drawn.

"Ramsey, sarge!" the corporal warned.

A shot rang out, the bullet cracking high into the air from the officer's gun as he slid from his saddle. The men remained mounted, eyes and guns raking over the empty terrain. After the thunder of hoofbeats, the snorting of weary horses and the creak of leather seemed like very tiny sounds scratching the silence.

"What's happening here?" the lieutenant demanded. "Don't shoot that man!"

Cuchillo saw the disgust in the eyes of the sergeant, then broke his gaze away from the stare to look at the lieutenant striding toward him. The officer was no older than the Apache. But he was a lot thinner and half a head shorter. From the pale complexion of his weakly handsome face, he had not been long under

34

the harsh sun of the southwest territories. By contrast with the burnished skin of his men, he looked positively unhealthy. There was nothing about his appearance to hint that he had the necessary hardness to command men. But the insignia on his dust-covered uniform gave him a certain degree of authority.

"Sergeant Duffy!" he snapped, stopping short of where the noncom held the Apache at his mercy. "I asked you a question!"

Lieutenant Ramsey's voice was stronger than his looks. And, up close, Cuchillo was able to see the unblinking determination in the officer's pale blue eyes. He decided that, even though the younger man did not have the same experience as the older, he could be as mean as the sergeant.

Duffy sighed and pulled himself erect, easing the muzzle of the Spencer away from Cuchillo's throat. "You can see what was done to the scout, sir," he reported. "This here Injun is the only one around. And he reckons he can take us to the ones that killed Hunter Man."

Ramsey moved in closer to Cuchillo, forcing the sergeant to back off. The blue eyes examined the Apache and continued to hold an expression of disgust that had sprung into them when he glanced at the mutilated body of the Mohave. After long moments, he glanced over his shoulder. "Sergeant Duffy, Corporal French, remain here. The rest of you men, take a look around." He waved his revolver over the rising and dipping terrain between the hill crest and the mouth of the gorge.

The men who had dismounted swung into their saddles and joined the others in urging their horses down the slope.

"Could I have water?" Cuchillo asked when Ramsey returned his attention to him.

"If you tell a good story, mister!" the lieutenant snapped in response. "What did you see, and how come you got left behind?"

In a deliberate attempt at mental torture, Duffy went to his horse, unhooked a canteen from the saddle, and uncapped it. He sucked a mouthful of water, swilled it around, and spat it out. It sizzled as it hit the the sun-heated rock.

"I was not with them," Cuchillo croaked. His cracked lips were painful and his tongue felt like a large wad of dry hide in his mouth. "I have traveled alone from far in the north. I reached that place over there." He turned and raised an arm to point toward the hill from where he had watched the first group of soldiers arrive at the outcrop.

"Was sure enough where he was hidin' when we showed up, sir," the corporal allowed.

He was as short as the sergeant, but didn't have any excess weight. About thirty, he had a very pointed nose and small eyes that gave him somewhat of a bird-like countenance.

"I was resting after my long journey,"

Cuchillo continued with his lies. "Voices speaking in my own tongue awoke me. I saw a band of Apache braves."

"Apaches are the worst Injuns of all," Duffy growled. This time he swallowed the water he sucked from the canteen.

There was shouting between the men scouring the country behind him, but Cuchillo did not turn around. He felt his eyes were locked in a trap with Ramsey's steady gaze.

"They were drunk with the firewater. They had bottles. Many bottles."

"How many of them?"

"Twenty at least."

"He talks English good and he can count!" Duffy growled. "Educated Apaches are worst of all."

"Keep your mouth shut!" Ramsey snapped over his shoulder.

The sergeant made a face at the back of the lieutenant.

"They heard you and your men approaching, lieutenant," Cuchillo went on. "Two were sent ahead to look for you. Soon, the Mohave came. He was captured and silently killed. Then many knives attacked his dead body. They rode quickly away, in the direction from which they came."

He turned now, to point at the gorge again. The soldiers had completed their search and were returning.

37

"I can track them for you."

"What did they look like?" The blue eyes had lost their look of horror. Suspicion lurked in them. But not of Cuchillo. The man's expression had changed when he heard that the Apaches were drunk and learned the number in the band. He supplemented the question. "Were they dressed like you?"

Cuchillo shook his head. Despite the pain and the tension, he had been able to rest. His vision was clearer, and so was his mind. He was able to consider more than one thought at a time, and provide a link between them. The horse-soldiers had been in a fight. They had lost their senior officer and maybe some other men—or else why the saddled horses hitched to the supplies wagon? Many of the drunken Apaches who had hunted him wore items of army clothing. "The clothes of the White Eyes," he reported as the searchers started back up the slope. "Some in the tunics and hats of soldiers. Others in the clothes of White Eyes not of the army." His voice was failing as talking further punished his parched throat. "Their chief, he carried the sword of a White Eyes army officer."

"Hot damn!" the corporal exclaimed. "Sir, they sure sound like the bunch that—"

"Give him a drink!" the lieutenant snapped, swinging toward the first group of returning soldiers.

"Trackin's gonna be hard over this kind of country, lieutenant," one of the men announced sourly. "Unless them Injuns mark their route with these."

He held up two empty whiskey bottles. Duffy made to bring his own canteen to Cuchillo, but changed his mind. He went to the horse of the dead Mohave and unhooked the canteen from the saddlehorn. He gave it to the Apache, who steeled himself against haste. Carefully, he uncapped the canteen, raised it to his lips, and tilted it by degrees. The water was tepid on his tongue, teeth, gums, and mouth lining. But it had the most delicious taste Cuchillo had ever savored. He swilled it about in his mouth, then allowed it to trickle down his throat. He gagged just once, then felt his body responding to the alleviating effects of its first intake of liquid for a seeming eternity.

As he continued to sip the life-giving water, he became aware of a new source of relief. He was shaded from the harsh glare of the sun. As he tipped water into the cupped palm of a hand and pressed it against his lips, he looked around him. All the soldiers had returned and were gathered around himself and the lieutenant. It was them and their horses providing the shade. There was talk, but Cuchillo was too concerned with relishing the relative comfort of his position to take note of what was being said. He did hear a series of crashing sounds as half-a-dozen whiskey bottles were hurled at the base of the outcrop and smashed into sun-glinting shards and splinters.

Then: "Okay, mister. You've bought yourself some time. On your feet and make use of it."

It was the lieutenant who spoke, his face set in a grim expression as he looked down at Cuchillo. The Apache climbed slowly to his feet. He swayed and his vision blurred. The water had done much to revive him, but he was a long way short of being at full strength. He needed food and rest to achieve this. Perhaps he would be able to eat, but the faces of the officer and his men warned that rest was far out of reach.

"You take the Mohave's horse," Ramsey instructed. "Your life depends upon you leading us to that party of renegade Apaches. So pull yourself together, mister!"

Sergeant Duffy spat. "Or you get taken apart," he growled.

CHAPTER THREE

Cuchillo chewed on strips of jerked beef and washed them down with swigs of water as he rode at the head of the advance group of soldiers. Distrust was like a tangible force emanating from each man and merging to push at him from behind. They were three miles from where the buzzards were adding further bloodied marks of mutilation to the body of the Mohave scout and, except for the burden of suspicion of him that Cuchillo sensed so strongly, he was feeling good.

In addition to water and food, he had also been supplied with a uniform shirt, tunic, and hat. The clothing kept the burning sun off his bare flesh. And the Mohave's gelding went some way to allowing him the rest he so urgently needed. The reason for the distrust was obvious. The quarry was a band of renegade Apaches who had broken free of a *rancheria*, under the influence of vast quantities of whiskey illicitly supplied by white traders. They had

41

murdered the traders, and an Indian agent, in the process of their breakout. The horsesoldiers had been assigned to bring back the Apaches—and had ridden into an ambush which cost the lives of the commanding major, a captain, and seven enlisted men.

Cuchillo had been told of this in spiteful tones by a man whose brother had been killed in the ambush. This while Lieutenant Ramsey organized his men into three groups. One, of forty men, including himself and Cuchillo, blazed the trail. Another group of twenty-five acted as a backup detachment, riding a half mile to the rear of the first. The remainder of the men acted as back-markers, primarily to guard the supplies wagon, and to act as reinforcements if necessary.

This splitting up of the column, in combination with murmurings of discontent, placed Cuchillo firmly under a cloud of suspicion. He was an Apache and had told a good story, which could be true or not. The concensus of opinion was definitely that he was a liar. It was possible—many of the men thought probable—that he was one of the renegade band: left behind with a rehearsed story so that he could lead the column into yet another ambush.

But three miles had been put behind the first group, and the sun had advanced halfway to the western horizon, without a sign of attack. And there had been many places where a surprise assault could have been launched. For, after they had bypassed the sheer rock wall of the gorge and Cuchillo had picked up the trail from where the Apache ponies had waited, the route was a tortuous one. Always west or southwest, cutting across hills and through canyons where every crest and every rim could have concealed many more than a score of Indians.

Tracking by visual sign was by turns difficult and simple. But, as the terrain slid by beneath them, an Apache of Cuchillo's skill was able to lead the cavalrymen at a fast and even pace. Confident they were not being followed, or recklessly drunk, the band of Apaches continued to drop their empty whiskey bottles. There were also the more conventional signs that a large group of horses had traversed the hill country. Dried and wet droppings and— where pockets of dust lay in rocky dips—the prints of unshod hooves.

Where there were no signs Cuchillo Oro, growing progressively stronger, tracked by instinct and logic. Ignoring the fact that the quarry were drunk, he kept in mind that they were Apaches. And not only that—they were also Mimbreños, like himself. Thus, when the country offered a choice of routes to the south and southwest, he elected to take the way which he would have chosen.

Evening was hovering on the edge of afternoon when he turned in the saddle, raised a finger to his lips, and reined the gelding to a halt. Lieutenant Ramsey imitated the action to bring the entire forward group of soldiers to a silent stop.

As the yellow glare of the sun lost some of its harshness by becoming tinged with red, all eyes were directed toward the mouth of a canyon a quarter of a mile ahead.

"I would like to scout there," Cuchillo said as Ramsey turned a quizzical gaze toward him.

"You saw something?" the lieutenant wanted to know.

"I see nothing. But I feel something about that place."

Sergeant Duffy spat and used a coat sleeve to wipe dusty sweat from his face. "Me too, sir," he growled. "That canyon looks like a fine place to bushwhack us."

He eyed Cuchillo from under lowered lids, making his meaning plain. The Apache sighed.

"I do not expect to be allowed to go alone. But I ask that no more than two men come with me. If there are more there would be no—"

"I'm aware of that, mister!" Ramsey snapped. "Duffy, French. Scout the canyon with the Apache."

The skinny corporal abruptly showed more suspicion than Duffy. "You reckon two's enough, sir?" he asked.

"Your yellow streak's showin', Frenchy,"

the sergeant rasped. "I can handle the Injun if he tries a double-cross."

"Head out!" Ramsey barked. He pulled a silver watch out of his pocket to check the time. "If I don't get a report in an hour, we'll advance."

The two noncoms saluted and then all three scouts heeled their mounts forward.

Ramsey called out after them: "Unless he tries anything, the Indian gives the orders!"

"Bastard shavetail!" Duffy rasped softly.

"I ain't yellow!" French whined.

Cuchillo ignored them as he led the way toward the canyon, keeping the pace to an easy canter and raking his narrow-eyed gaze over their objective. The canyon cut like the wound from a gigantic cleaver into a hillside. The mouth was narrow and low-walled, with a fall of rocks heaped at one side. Deeper in, it appeared to broaden, as the walls grew higher and sheer. There was a choice of scouting methods—either directly into the canyon or a climb up the hill to survey it from above. He chose the latter and elected to proceed on foot. As the trio tethered their horses among the rockfall, Duffy and French growled their discontent.

"Never figured I'd see the day I'd take orders from a friggin' Apache!" the sergeant muttered.

"If I liked walkin' I'd have joined the damn infantry!" the corporal countered.

"If Cuchillo wanted noise, he would take horses, not White Eyes," the Apache said pointedly.

They started to climb, as the sun grew even more red and spread a pink glow across the western dome of the sky.

"He tellin' us to keep our mouths shut?" French asked.

"Man, I hate Apaches," Duffy said, and left it at that.

"Cuchillo?" French mused as they climbed higher, all three of them sweating with the exertion, despite the fact that the sinking sun was losing its heat. "That don't sound like no Apache name."

"It's Mex," Duffy supplied between deep, gulping breaths. His bulky build did not suit him to climbing. "Means knife."

Cuchillo halted suddenly, halfway to the top of the steepening rise. He swung around to face the two soldiers. They were pulled up sharply, and made to level their Spencers.

"Cuchillo Oro," the Apache hissed, his expression heavy with mean, controlled anger. "Both are from the Spanish language which the Mexicans speak. The meaning of my name in your tongue is Golden Knife." He reached down to his right legging, slackened the two tight thongs, and drew out the *cinquedea*. Because of Ramsey's distrust of him, he had not been given a gun and the knife was still his sole

46

weapon. Both noncoms eyed the ornate knife with surprise, then avariciousness. "I was named first because I was skilled with knife. Got next name when I get this." He thrust the knife into his waistband and unbuttoned the tunic. "Not time or place to tell you rest of my life story."

"Sassy Injun, ain't he?" French said. "And sneaky—carryin' that hidden blade."

"I hate Apaches!" Duffy recited.

Cuchillo shot a glance down the slope, toward where the first group of backup soldiers were closing with the advance party. Then he swung around and continued the climb. Indulging spite, he set a faster pace, but soon he had to slow it. Duffy suffered most from the extra exertion, but French's mutterings were as noisy as the sergeant's wheezy breathing.

The sun had hidden half its bulk below the horizon by the time they attained the three hundred foot high crest of the hill. In the failing light of day's end, the silence seemed to become heavier and more brittle. The two soldiers were suddenly conscious of the noise they were making and at last became aware of how dangerous it could be. They did their best to match the stealth of Cuchillo Oro as all three crawled on their bellies toward the western rim of the canyon's highest wall. But this was not possible, because they were not of the Apache breed.

Cuchillo reached the vantage point first, and

swung his head around to show the soldiers a finger to his lips. They bellied up on either side of him and peered downward. They blinked beads of sweat off their eyelids and saw the Apaches they had traveled so far to find.

The entire party of renegades was down there, resting in the deep shade of the canyon wall. The majority were asleep, sprawled out on their blankets. In what would otherwise have been complete silence, the sounds of their deep breathing and stentorian snoring rose up to the ears of the watchers. Four braves were on sentry duty but weariness and liquor caused their heads to droop as they squatted in the cool shade, two at either side of the resting group. The ponies, more beat than the Indians, were hobbled within the area under careless guard.

Duffy and French both tilted their rifles over the canyon rim to draw beads on the Apaches immediately below them.

"Reckon we could blast six of 'em before the rest knew what the hell was happenin'," the sergeant whispered.

"Hot damn, yeah," the corporal agreed.

Cuchillo expressed silent disgust—for the soldiers and for the Apache sentries. Any Indian with his wits about him would have detected the distant sound of voices. Cuchillo himself would have sensed the presence of intruders nearby. He bellied back from the edge of the cliff until he was able to stand erect. Reluctantly, Duffy and French did likewise. They could not see Lieutenant Ramsey and the men from their position and Cuchillo toyed with the idea of sending one of the noncoms back with the message. But he rejected it at once, knowing the men would put up an argument and that he would lose it—losing time in the process and perhaps alerting the Apaches down below.

Using hand signals, he instructed the two soldiers to follow him and led them along the canyon rim, beyond the point where the Apaches were camped. The sun was almost completely set and more than half the allotted hour had been used when he reached a place where they could climb down into the canyon—with relative ease and without the danger of making enough sound to alert the Apaches.

His thirst slaked, with food in his belly, and some of his strength returned, Cuchillo climbed with fast agility. The soldiers dropped down into the canyon with bad grace and diminished stamina. The cliff face was far from sheer now, and featured with countless niches to provide steps down to the floor. A slight kink in the canyon hid their progress from the Apaches but all were aware that the walls would channel noise back toward the camp. So, despite their ill-humor, the two soldiers took great care not to dislodge loose pieces of rock and pebbles.

"What now, master-mind?" Duffy rasped as he and French reached the foot of the cliff, some ten minutes after Cuchillo had made it.

"You have time piece?" the Apache asked.

"Only damn officers need them!" French growled.

Cuchillo pointed to the many vertical clefts cut into the rock at the foot of each facing cliff. "Officer say he will wait one hour. Now we wait in hiding until that time gone. Renegades may stay to fight, but soldiers are many. They will run, at first or later. This only way to run."

Duffy and French were both veteran soldiers who had not earned their chevrons merely by length of service. They had seen action in the war back east and had done their share of Indian-fighting since being assigned to duty in the southwestern territories. Their eyes expressed tacit and grudging approval for the Apache's plan.

"One on one side and two on other," Cuchillo augmented. "Be better if I have gun."

Duffy spat. "I don't want to be havin' to watch you as well as the rest of them Injuns," he muttered.

"Hey, sarge," French argued. "He's right. When them Apaches hear Ramsey leadin' the boys up the canyon, they'll likely up and come runnin' first thing. Twenty Injuns are gonna take a lot of blastin'. Another gun'll make a big difference."

Duffy knew this and his eyes showed it.

"Why the hell should he turn on us, hot

damn?" French encouraged, unfastening his holster flap.

"We ain't exactly made ourselves buddies with him." Then he sighed. "Okay, give him your iron, French. But I want him between me and the rest of the friggin' Injuns."

The corporal gave Cuchillo his Colt and a handful of spare ammunition. With the rene-gades trapped between the unequal forces of their pursuers, Duffy assumed command from Cuchillo. He directed the Apache to a hiding place just around the slight turn in the canyon. French was sent to the opposite side. Duffy himself pressed into a cleft twenty yards be-hind Cuchillo's position.

Then there was nothing to do except wait as the shadows from the sun were replaced by the encroaching darkness of night.

Cuchillo checked the action of the revolver, holding it in his good, left hand. After his first, abortive attempt upon the life of the hated Pinner, he had spent a long time in the barren mountains of Sonora, training himself to be-come as skilled in the use of his left hand as he always had been with his right. Not to use it for mundane acts—instead for the business of killing. And he had taught himself well. With revolver, rifle, knife, tomahawk, lance, and bow he was as good a warrior now as he had ever been before his hand was tortured into near uselessness. Better even, because there had been many opportunities to put his skills to the test. Before that fateful day when Pinner had ordered him dragged from the borderline *rancheria,* shaming him before every brave and squaw who lived there, Cuchillo had killed only game. But the false accusation and unjust punishment had drawn from him a response of retaliation that had made him as much of a renegade as the Apaches for whom he now waited.

So far, his desire for vengeance was unsatisfied. But many had fallen by his hand to mark red the trail that had brought him to this canyon in the fast falling night. He had been forced to kill often and his left hand had never let him down: forced to kill to stay alive and continue the hunt for Pinner.

The distant beat of hoofbeats trembled the cooling air and he eased back the hammer of the Colt. He was going to kill again and the reason was the same. Every Apache camped along the canyon was going to have to die, for if just a single prisoner was taken, the survivor's word might be accepted against that of Cuchillo.

Shouts of alarm sounded above the beat of hooves. A gun cracked, but probably in warning rather than battle.

"Get ready, Injun!" Duffy yelled. "I wanna see you blastin' at them murderin' bastards."

A fusillade of shots sounded, drowning out

the notes of a bugle wailing the charge. Cuchillo set the lines of his face into an expression of grim determination. The danger of allowing a prisoner to be taken lost its significance in his mind. Instead, he recalled his agonies as the renegades made sport out of pursuing him. He recalled his parched throat, his bursting lungs, and his aching muscles. He thought about the despair at dying with his mission uncompleted as he lay coiled in the depression, watching his tormentors advance up the slope.

He squeezed the Colt's trigger. The rifles of Duffy and French exploded at precisely the same moment as the revolver fired.

Three braves died. They were at the head of the retreat, racing their ponies at a flat-out gallop around the gentle turn in the canyon. They were half-turned, staring back at their pursuers. The bullets plunged into their chests and they were lifted from the backs of their mounts. Spraying droplets of blood through the rising dust, they twisted in mid-air and thudded to the ground. The braves behind them snapped their heads to the front and began to rein in their ponies.

One horse stumbled on a crumpled body and pitched the rider over his head and neck. Duffy and French chose the brave for their target and exploded two bullets toward him. One found his thigh and he screamed. The second burrowed through an eye into his brain and silenced him before he crashed to the ground.

Cuchillo's revolver spat death, and found a mark. A pony, rearing as he was reined to a skidding halt, took the bullet in his throat. He spasmed to his end, contorting his body and tipping his rider clear. The brave hit the ground and was crushed to a pulp beneath the crashing carcass.

Guns, like heads, were swung toward the front, and a hail of bullets replied to the opening fire of Cuchillo and the two soldiers. But the first fusillade was a reckless response to the unexpected. The Apaches thought they had been cut off by a large force of soldiers and they directed their fire toward every possible place of concealment.

Corporal French was hit in the shoulder and the impact of the bullet spun him out of his cover. He was seen and three braves leapt from their skidding ponies and sprinted toward him, exploding shots at him. French was hit in the other shoulder and thrown back against the canyon wall. He bounced away and dropped on to his knees. He triggered off a bullet and a brave pulled up, clutched at a blossoming crimson stain at his stomach and corkscrewed to the ground. French was hit twice more, blood spurting from his thigh and forearm.

"Who's friggin' yellow, Duffy, you bastard!" he screamed, pumping the action of the Spencer and squeezing the trigger in quick succession.

The other two running braves were stopped in their tracks, both taking chest wounds that spun them before dropping them. The remainder of the renegades had heeled their ponies forward again, knowing that whatever awaited them in front could be no worse than the mass of cavalry approaching from the rear.

French got off one more shot before a bullet found his heart and he crumpled back against the canyon wall. Cuchillo emptied the revolver of live shells and started to reload. Duffy picked his targets and snapped off shots toward them with cool calmness. Loose ponies raced around the turn in the canyon, signs that the barrage of fire from Ramsey and his men was having a deadly effect on the renegades.

Rock splinters showered Cuchillo and he snapped up his head from reloading the Colt. The chief was swerving his pony toward the cleft, hatred seeming to physically drip from his face as he blasted off shots from a revolver. The gun rattled empty and the man drew the stolen saber from his belt. He lifted it high above his head, as if to throw it.

But a saber was not a throwing weapon. The chief released the reins of his pony and launched himself clear of the animal's back. He landed, evenly balanced, with agile grace, and lunged into a run toward Cuchillo. The saber went to the side, then started to descend.

"Apache traitor!" the chief bellowed above the raucous noise of the battle. "You die!"

Cuchillo had been able to eject the spent cartridges, but there were no live rounds in the chambers of the Colt. He dropped the gun and dove a hand under his unbuttoned tunic. The knife came free and was hurled in a single, fluid action. The chief had closed within four feet of Cuchillo and the saber was swinging fast for a vicious slash at the side of his neck.

The knife sank to its hilt in the stomach of the chief. But he still lived. The saber kept coming as he fell forward, pain mixed with hatred on his features. Cuchillo threw his arm high, acting as a bar. The chief's forearm met his with terrific force. Cuchillo snapped up his knee and slammed it into the face of his attacker. He heard the smashing of bone and saw blood explode from either side of the pulped nose. The chief fell, releasing the saber.

Cuchillo, his pulse racing, stooped to pick up the Colt. But the dying chief was lying on it. He grasped the saber instead, as bullets spattered against the rocks around him. He looked through the billowing dust and drifting gunsmoke, his flared nostrils filled with the stench of burnt powder and blood. He saw many slumped bodies but there was no time for a count. Ponies continued to gallop from around the turn in the canyon, not all of them riderless.

With a single cut of the saber, he decapitated the chief.

"Hey, that's a pretty mean scalpin', injun!" Duffy yelled, witnessing the culmination of Cuchillo's revenge against the man who had ordered the torment of the morning.

Then the sergeant grunted and fell back, dropping the Spencer he was in the process of reloading. Blood spurted from his chest, right of center.

Five braves, roaring their triumph, raced their ponies through the stampede of riderless mounts, aware they had broken from the trap. The thunder of shod hooves rose in volume, but no soldier had yet ridden into sight around the canyon's turn.

Cuchillo hurled the saber with its grisly burden across the body-littered canyon and sprinted out of his cleft toward where Duffy writhed and groaned on the ground.

"Hell, do I hate Apaches!" the sergeant roared as Cuchillo snatched up the Spencer.

"Cuchillo not fond of some," the Indian allowed as he thudded the rifle stock to his shoulder and dropped to one knee.

He began to squeeze the trigger and work the repeater action. Duffy had managed to feed only five live shells into the magazine. They were enough. The range started out at forty yards for the first of the five escaping Apaches to die. Cuchillo held the rifle in rock-steady hands, swinging it along the line of riders and plunging a .30 caliber bullet into each of them. The first two were hit in the back. The other three turned, the sounds of their triumph fading. The third man to die was holed in the head. The other two faced front again, kicking feet and slapping hands demanding greater speed from their ponies. One took a bullet in the nape of his neck and the last brave to die, at a range of more than a hundred and fifty yards, was only wounded by a bullet in the shoulder. But the shot toppled him sideways off his horse and he smashed his skull against the canyon wall.

"You ain't all mouth, injun," Duffy groaned as Ramsey rode at the head of the men around the turn, skidding his horse to a rearing halt and yelling for the entire squad to do likewise. "I'll say that for you."

Three riderless army horses galloped on down the canyon, showing that Corporal French had not been the only White Eyes casualty. The mounted men surveyed the litter of dead Apaches with grim satisfaction.

"Any of the hostiles get away?" Ramsey demanded.

"Not a one of 'em, sir," Duffy reported, grimacing with the pain from his wound.

"How did the Indian acquit himself, sergeant?"

Duffy eyed Cuchillo with an expression akin to respect. "I'd say he did okay, sir."

Ramsey saw the severed head with the saber still sunk into the gory neck. He dismounted and there were signs of threatened nausea on his pale face as he crossed to where the head lay. He put a boot on it and withdrew the saber. "This was Major Yancy's," he announced absently. He used the blood-dripping point to prod the head as Cuchillo allowed the Spencer to fall and crossed to the body of the chief. "What is this barbarous act supposed to prove?" the lieutenant demanded of Duffy.

Cuchillo used a foot to roll the chief over on his back. He stooped and pulled out the golden knife. He wiped the blade on the coat sleeve of the dead man before thrusting the knife into his waistband.

Duffy shrugged, and winced at the pain the action caused. "I wouldn't know, sir." Then he grinned. "But these educated Injuns—do some real crazy things to get ahead."

CHAPTER FOUR

Fort Wylie was sited in the eastern foothills of the Dragoon Mountains, almost a hundred miles north of the border territory that Cuchillo knew so well. But, given a choice by Ramsey to continue his homeward trek or stay with the horsesoldiers, the Apache elected to accept the latter. Particularly since the offer was combined with a half-promise that he could have a job as scout.

It took all of the following day to reach the fort, after the soldiers had camped the night in the canyon mouth, away from the stench of decomposing bodies. And during the long ride under the hot sun, Cuchillo considered the twin advantages attached to his decision.

Firstly, he would have a job for which he would be paid and there would also be food and shelter. For a lone Apache banished by his tribe and regarded with distrust by the White Eyes, this was luxury indeed. Secondly—and by far the most important—he would be part of the same army in which Captain Cyrus L. Pinner served. And if a man was trying to find another, it was far easier to search from the inside than from the out: particularly if one was trusted on the inside and regarded with constant suspicion on the out.

Thus, when Cuchillo saw Fort Wylie in the fading light at the end of another day, he viewed it with spirits that were gently buoyant. The obvious fact that, if the job as army scout made it easier for him to find Pinner, the same principle would also work in reverse, did not subdue his mood. A man was unlikely to win anything if he was not prepared to risk anything—in some cases, everything.

The fort was well situated and strongly built. It stood on a flattened hilltop, that seemed to have been leveled off by the tools of man rather than the ravages of nature. Although the column approached it from high ground, the men had to drop down into a dry, natural moat and climb a steep slope to reach the fort. The higher hill provided a vantage point, but was out of rifle range and when the column was on a level with the fort, they had a further quarter of a mile to cover before they reached the gate.

From his first view of the fort, Cuchillo had seen that it was built of both brick and timber, on conventional stockade lines. Each of the four walls was comprised of thirty foot high lengths of timber, spiked at the top and with sentry walks behind them. At each corner was a brick-built tower. None of the buildings behind the walls were built close to them. Instead, the administration block, bunkhouses, officers' quarters, stables, arms store, cook house, and other accommodations were grouped at the center of the compound. Thus, if attackers managed to cross the surrounding open ground and scale the high walls, there was no easy access down via rooftops.

As the head of the column neared the big double gates which swung open to admit them, Cuchillo sensed the lightening moods of the returning men. And he could understand this. They had been out in the wilderness of the barren hills for two nights and almost three days. They had been engaged in two battles with the renegade Apaches and had lost several men. Even after their quarry had been wiped out, there was no guarantee that other marauding Indians would not try to ambush them. In contrast to discomfort, the constant threat of death and death itself, the opening gates of Fort Wylie offered access to a minor paradise.

Darkness had fallen completely while the column covered the final stretch and the bright, welcoming glow of lamps showed in the gap of the gateway. The aroma of cooking food struggled through the acrid taint of smoke from the stoves on which the evening meal was being prepared.

"Glad to have you back, sir!" one of the gate sentries called, throwing up a salute that was as smart as his uniform was neat and clean.

"You get them lousy bastards, lieutenant?" the man on the second gate wanted to know.

Ramsey swung a look of harsh authority from one man to the other. "If either of you men happened to be commanding officer of Fort Wylie, you'd be the first to know!" he snapped.

Then the head of the column was through the gateway. There was no breaking of ranks as Ramsey led them into a disheveled parade ground formation in front of the fort office, on the stoop of which a colonel stood waiting. From whispered comments spoken by soldiers toward the back of the column, the gate sentries received a virtually full report of action out in the hills. And, even before the lieutenant received permission from his commanding officer to dismiss the men, the story was circulated.

All the hostiles were dead; the two senior officers and several men were just as dead; so was the Mohave scout; but they had picked up an Apache replacement; Duffy, who was pretty badly wounded, reckoned the Apache was okay.

Every man—soldier and civilian, on and off duty—had watched the return of the travel and battle-weary column. And, as the piecemeal story of their experiences was circulated, Cuchillo Oro became a main focus of attention.

He sensed this, and glanced around the interior of the stockade as he waited beside Lieutenant Ramsey for the backmarkers of the column to join the formation. In the lamplight, which shone through windows and dropped from lanterns lashed to the tops of poles, he examined the faces of the onlookers. A few showed the familiar hatred he had come to expect from White Eyes. A great many more expressed simple curiosity. One—the most attractive of all—was turned toward him with a look of deep interest.

It was the only woman in sight, which could well mean she was the only woman at the fort. She stood in the doorway of the saddler's store, her slender body silhouetted against the light from behind her and her face lit from a lamp which flickered above the open door. She was about twenty-five, with large, dark eyes dominating features which were a handsome blend from the heritage of two races—a half-breed.

Other faces and forms stood out from the crowd of watchers. The man who lounged beside the woman, matched her height of a little over five feet. The expression on his rat-like face contrasted starkly with the look she was giving Cuchillo. This man generated a bitter hatred toward the Apache. Then, in front of a crudely built shack at the side of a bunkhouse, a trio of Mohave scouts eyed Cuchillo with a mixture of coldness and anxiety. The stoutly built, gray-haired colonel viewed the stranger with complete indifference.

"Arrange for the wounded to be taken care of, then dismiss the men, lieutenant," the commanding officer barked when the gates had been heavily closed after the supplies wagon and its complement of riderless horses had entered the fort. "Then come in and deliver your report."

Ramsey relayed the orders to the men and matched their actions of swinging from his saddle. He pressed the reins of his horse into the hands of a sergeant.

"There is place for me?" Cuchillo asked, still in the saddle.

"That I don't know, mister," Ramsey answered. "I made you an offer, not a promise. I'll put in a word for you with Colonel Zentner."

"I just wait here?"

Ramsey jerked a thumb toward where the Mohaves stood. "That's the scout quarters. Stable the horse, then wait in there. Someone will let you know, one way or the other."

He spun around and strode smartly toward the doorway into which the colonel had disappeared. The fort was abruptly noisy and filled with movement again after the quiet interlude of the short parade. Cuchillo became just one of the crowd as he dismounted and led the gelding into the stable. Accepted by the men he had scouted for and fought with, he was readily advised on which was the gelding's stall and where to store the saddle and other gear.

It was the driver of the supplies wagon, who had done a great deal of talking with the wounded Duffy on the long haul back to Fort Wylie, who offered Cuchillo some extra advice. He was a sergeant himself, a bearded man nearing the age when he would face compulsory discharge from the army. He grasped Cuchillo's arm as the Apache was about to leave the stable. Cuchillo pulled up sharply, his frame becoming rigid as his muscles tensed to retaliate against an unprovoked attack.

The elderly noncom let go of the arm as though it had suddenly become red hot. "Hey, mate!" he said nervously. "You're with friends. Some, anyway."

The stiffness went out of the Apache. "You wish something from Cuchillo?"

The sergeant smiled, showing a lot of rotten teeth amongst a few good ones. But Cuchillo, who found it as difficult to trust the White Eyes as they did him, kept his expression impassive.

"Just wanted to give you a warnin', is all."

"I am listening."

The sergeant bit at a plug of tobacco and began to chew it noisily. "Mate, you sure make it hard to be friends," he growled.

"Friendship like money—must be earned," the Apache answered flatly.

"So, go to hell, Injun!" the sergeant muttered, and spat out a stream of tobacco juice. He started to turn away, to join the other soldiers heading out of the stable toward the cookhouse with its appetizing smell of hot food.

"Easy money·is not good," Cuchillo said.

"Speak for yourself," the sergeant countered, but held back as he saw a flicker of warmth in the coldness of the Indian's dark eyes. "Just don't mess with Mary Neat."

The dark eyes blinked.

"Only female on this godforsaken post," the sergeant augmented. "You must have seen her outside the saddler's store. She was seein' you, sure enough."

"Cuchillo not look for trouble."

Another stream of tobacco juice hit the door frame of the stable. With more force this time. "Where that dame's concerned, mate, you got to keep lookin' for trouble—to duck outta the way when it comes."

Cuchillo was suddenly impatient. The stable was heady with the stench of horse sweat, rotting straw, and fresh droppings. But the aroma of food was strong enough to cut across this and stir his gastric juices by way of his flared nostrils. "You talk in the riddles of the White Eyes," he said irritably.

The final group of weary and hungry soldiers left the stable and the sergeant and the Indian were alone, with all the lamps turned low. The noncom sighed.

"I'll spell it out for you, mate. Bill Neat—that was the skinny guy standin' next to Mary—is the woman's Pa. Long time ago, he got himself mixed up with an Apache squaw. Some reckoned he was married to her and some say not. Whatever, the squaw had a brat, and the brat growed up to be Mary. Ain't no one knows what happened to her mother. But, whatever, she must have been a fine-lookin' woman, 'cause Mary sure enough didn't get to be the looker she is from that bastard Neat."

"Longer the story, the blunter is the point," Cuchillo muttered, coining another of the aphorisms he was wont to voice at the slightest opportunity.

"I'm gettin' to it, I'm gettin' to it, mate," the sergeant growled with irritation. "Neat's got high hopes for that daughter of his. Wants her to marry a white man. Rich-type white man. Officer type. Which is why he hauls her around the army posts all over this neck-of-the-woods." Tobacco juice hit the door frame. "But that woman, she has different ideas. Ain't only her looks she got more from her Ma than Pa. She figures to get herself hitched to an Injun."

He looked pointedly at Cuchillo.

"This Indian has no plans for a squaw."

The sergeant shrugged. "Lots of women have changed the minds of a whole lot of men about that, mate. And Mary Neat's got the face and build that goes a long way to doin' the changin'. But it ain't exactly her female wiles I'm warnin' you about. We used to have five Mohave scouts at this post. That woman set her cap at one of 'em and he fell for her. Then Bill Neat found 'em together out back of the guardhouse. Weren't doin' nothin' but walkin' and talkin'."

"White Eyes kill Mohave?" Cuchillo asked flatly.

The sergeant grimaced. "Didn't make it that easy for the Injun. Knocked him out, then broke both his legs and both his arms. After that, the Injun wasn't no use for scoutin'. Wasn't no use for much at all."

Cuchillo nodded, as the tone of finality in the sergeant's voice indicated he had concluded his story. "I thank you for the warning. We can eat now?"

The sergeant sighed and moved into the stable doorway. "I'm sure gonna eat, mate. Dunno what that shavetail lieutenant fixed for you."

He ambled outside and across the compound toward the cook house, which was noisy with the sound of eating and talk. Cuchillo went out of the stable and now he sensed just one watcher. The only men in sight once the sergeant had disappeared were the sentries patroling the wooden walkways at the top of the stockade walls. Their attention was focused on the moonlit hills surrounding the fort.

He turned to the left and moved across the front of the stable block toward the scouts' quarters. To reach his objective he had to pass in front of the saddler's store. The sense of being under surveillance strengthened as he neared the open doorway. The lamp inside the store had been extinguished, but that above it continued to drop a cone of light.

"I hear of your bravery, Cuchillo Oro," a woman's voice whispered.

He halted, directly under the lamp. Lightly shod feet moved across the floorboards within the store and Mary Neat emerged on to the threshold. He saw her more clearly than previously, her face and body displayed in the fringe glow from the lamp. She was even more beautiful than at first glance, with only the paleness of her complexion to betray the white blood which coursed through her veins. She had the flat forehead, high cheekbones, flared nose, and full lips of an Apache squaw—the whole framed by jet black hair that fell down her back with no hint of a wave. Her slender body, with small, pert breasts and a narrow waist, was clothed in a tight-fitting dress of pale green that hid her flesh but not her lines from throat to ankles. It had the look of a gown that had been expensive to buy, but it had suffered a great deal of hard wearing. She spoke English in a way that indicated it was not her native tongue.

"Stories told at secondhand are often of no

value," he answered, nodding in response to her quiet smile.

"You will place no value on the stories you have heard about me?" Humor showed in her dark eyes.

"How do you know I have heard of you?"

Her gaze looked beyond Cuchillo, sweeping around the fort. "I am the only woman in Fort Wylie. I know that I am spoken of often."

Despite what the sergeant had told him about Mary Neat and her father, Cuchillo felt himself sexually attracted to the woman. As a female in an otherwise exclusively male world, she recognized the signs. And she offered tacit encouragement. Her smile became one of invitation and she darted out a tongue to delicately moisten her lips, causing them to shine in the lamplight. She half turned and sucked in a deep breath, to emphasize the line of her breasts and place the curves of the twin mounds into profile.

"Hey, you!"

The voice rang out across the compound. In the cook house, the noise of many men eating their meal continued. But the sentries atop the walkways heard the shout. And, like Cuchillo and Mary, they swung to look toward Bill Neat. He was coming from the latrine, still buttoning the front of his pants as he hurried across toward his store.

"My father can be brutal towards weak-

71

hearted men who show interest in me," the woman challenged softly.

"Cuchillo is not weak in any way," the Apache answered, pointedly not commenting on the latter half of her taunt.

"I don't want no filthy savage sniffin' around my gal!" the saddler snarled.

His pants were buttoned now, and he broke out of the ungainly walk into a loping run. Cuchillo eyed him indifferently, resisting the impulse to consider Neat as a no-account little man with a big mouth. And this not simply because of the warnings he had received from the bearded sergeant and Neat's daughter. The man was small, sure enough, in regard to his build—a head and shoulders shorter than Cuchillo and lacking weight in either fat or muscular development. But what he lacked in physique was compensated for in cunning, the Apache decided. It showed in the saddler's small, deepset blue eyes, which were angry, but watchful, as he slowed his approach toward Cuchillo and Mary. And there was grim determination in the set of his thin slash of a mouth. He was dressed in new leather boots and old and work-stained denim pants and shirt. There was a holstered Remington revolver on his belt, not tied-down, with the gun butt jutting above his right hipbone. He was unshaven, with face and hands still grimed from a day's work.

"I think maybe you as filthy as me, White

Eyes," Cuchillo responded softly, aware of the watching sentries. "But I had no chance to clean myself since coming to this place."

Neat was halted six feet from where the Apache stood. The taunt caused him to become rigid. He clenched his fists and his skin was abruptly purple beneath the grime.

"Don't you talk back to me, Injun!" he snarled.

"You started talk."

"Father, he was doing no harm!" Mary cut in, but her anxiety had a false ring.

"Keep outta this, gal!" Neat barked at her. "And get inside. I told you a hundred times about encouragin' savages like him."

Cuchillo did not consider himself perfect. He had many faults and one of the worst of these was his volatile temper. Learning to control it was a far harder task than schooling himself to use his left hand after the right was made useless. But, as a last resort, he always recalled the words of John Hedges, the only White Eyes he called a friend. Hedges had been a tutor at the borderline *rancheria* and Cuchillo had been his star pupil. The teacher had imparted to the pupil more than the contents of books.

"You're an Apache," John Hedges had once said when Cuchillo was little more than a boy and over-anxious to achieve warrior status. *"This is Apache land, but the white men have*

*claimed it and they will hold it by force of
their numbers, if nothing else. They feel guilty
for having stolen what they hold and they will
hate and revile the Apaches to appease their
consciences. But you must try to ignore their
acts of hatred, Cuchillo. If they refuse to be
ignored, use words before force. In big trouble,
the white men will always win because of the
force of numbers. Big trouble begins with small.
Always try to talk your way out of the small
trouble and thereby avoid losing the final, large
argument."*

"I think maybe," Cuchillo said, his voice
taut, "that to break arms and legs of uncon-
scious man is savage."

Neat had a bad temper of his own, and the
new barb almost drew it out into the open.
But he, also, could exercise self-control. "Get
lost, Injun!" he barked, starting forward in a
curve to walk around Cuchillo and reach the
doorway in which the woman continued to
stand. "And keep your nose away from my gal
and outta my business. Get me?"

Mary was genuinely afraid now, and she
backed into the store as her father reached the
doorway. Cuchillo glimpsed her face just before
she withdrew from out of the lamplight. It
expressed blatant scorn, directed toward him.
He recalled another man's words now. Those of
the elderly sergeant telling him that he didn't
have to look for trouble with Mary Neat, but to

duck out of the way when she brought it to him.

He started to turn away, his pride hurt by having to submit to the diminutive White Eyes: and his manhood injured by the contempt the woman felt for him. But trouble was a threat to the job he had a good chance of getting—a job that could lead him to the completion of his mission of vengeance against Pinner.

"See that, gal?" Neat announced rhetorically, the tone of his voice as filled with contempt as the eyes of his daughter had been. "That's why I want you to marry an officer and a gentlemen. These filthy savages are all the same. Regular hellcats when they're in a bunch. On their own, they won't stand up to a white man more than double their age."

The challenge brought Cuchillo's temper to the surface. He immediately forgot every word of advice John Hedges had ever given him: and he ignored the reason why he had come to Fort Wylie. He halted and whirled around to face his accuser. But he did nothing more reckless than this. For he had managed to conquer one dangerous aspect of his temper. It was never hot and blind anymore. He could demand satisfaction and seek to achieve it with cool calculation and unimpaired senses.

Had rage been boiling inside him, he would have died at that moment. For Neat had drawn the Remington as Cuchillo turned. The hammer was cocked and the muzzle drew a bead on the Apache's chest. If Cuchillo had taken one step toward Neat, the little man would have squeezed the trigger. It showed in the grim line of his mouth as his eyes extended a tacit invitation to make the move.

"You threatenin' me, Injun?" Neat rasped.

The golden knife was concealed by Cuchillo's tunic. But Corporal French's Colt, which he had been allowed to keep after the fight in the canyon, was in plain sight jutting from its holster.

"Bare hands against a gun?" Cuchillo hissed.

Neat grinned and slid the Remington back into his holster. He adopted the gunfighter's stance—feet apart and body twisted slightly from the waist to narrow the target. "Both got an even chance at the draw now, Injun," he challenged.

Confidence oozed from the smaller man and Cuchillo was faced with the prospect of having to back down a second time. Or die. He could shoot accurately, but he was not fast on the draw. From Neat's attitude, it was obvious he was an expert in both skills. The distance between the two men was ten feet and that needed to be halved if Cuchillo was to have a chance to jump Neat.

"Don't listen to him, mate," a familiar voice called. And there was another familiar sound—

of tobacco juice spattered against something solid.

The elderly sergeant called the warning across the compound from the cook house doorway. Cuchillo had his back toward that direction and kept his gaze fixed upon Neat's face. Neat, sensing that Cuchillo would be quick to spot an opening, also refused to look away.

"Right enough, feller!" one of the guards called down from the walkway at one side of the gate. His voice rang out more clearly than that of the sergeant, for the noise from the cook house had subsided. Then followed the sound of chair legs scraping on floorboards, and fast-moving footfalls. Cuchillo sensed many eyes upon him again. "He's an expert in more ways than one of hurtin' a man," the sentry continued. "Gotta be, on account of havin' to ride herd on that cock-teasin' daughter of his!"

This insult at Mary broke through Neat's self-control. It happened in less than a second, but Cuchillo saw each component part of the whole. The blue eyes caught fire, the lips curled back in a snarl, the body stiffened and turned, the hand went for the gun, and the head snapped around. The only sound was the start of an animalistic growl.

Then, the moment Neat's eyes were turned away from Cuchillo, peering through the darkness between the pools of lamplight, the Apache made his move. First he powered into two strides of a run, then altered his posture to launch himself into a dive. The Remington was clear of the holster by then, but Neat was no longer concerned with the sentry's insult. He had sensed, heard, and then seen Cuchillo powering toward him. But his gun hand was a fraction of a second later than his eyes in swinging toward the Apache.

Cuchillo did not try reaching for the Remington. The odds against making a grasping connection were too long. Instead, he splayed and then curled his arms, to hook his hands around the back of Neat. His body was in mid-air, stretched out at full-length, when he got a grip on the sparse flesh of the man's back. An instant later, he thudded the top of his head into Neat's stomach.

Neat's gun hand was outside the curve of Cuchillo's arm and he tried to force the Remington around to get a shot at the Apache. But the head butt was too powerful to ride with and Neat's will and strength left him as fast as the rush of air from his open mouth.

"Wonderful!" Mary whispered excitedly from the darkness of the saddler's store, her voice counter-pointing the grunt of pain.

Cuchillo thudded his feet to the ground and kept his hands locked behind Neat's back and his head hard against the man's stomach. Neat's doubled-over form started to be hurled backward by the force of the butt. But abruptly, as

Cuchillo's feet hit the ground and he straightened, the smaller man was whipped high into the air: draped over the head of the towering Apache. He flailed his arms and the Remington was jerked free. The gun sailed through the air, clunked against the front of the store, and dropped to the ground.

The Apache began to spin and Neat's torso and legs were flung out into an almost straight line as he was turned. Cuchillo saw many faces. It seemed that every soldier in the fort had emerged on to the compound to witness the contest. And, from their grinning faces, it was obvious how they felt about it: they were enjoying the sight of Bill Neat's suffering and humiliation.

Cuchillo did not throw his victim. He merely released his grip on him, ducked his head and stepped out from under the man. Neat's cry of alarm was the only sound in Fort Wylie, for the audience had remained utterly silent, except for the woman's single word of excited consent. His form still spinning at full-stretch, Neat crashed face-down to the hard ground. His groan of pain was just a little louder than the thud of the impact. He rolled over on to his back and began to gasp for breath as he clawed at his stomach and stared with bulging eyes up at the dark sky.

"Be thankful you are of many years,"

Cuchillo told the man on the ground. "If not, you would have died a young man."

He looked up from Neat and saw Mary, who had advanced to the threshold of the store again. In the light from above, her eyes glinted and her teeth gleamed in an expression of pure delight. Then he spun around and started toward the scouts' quarters. The eyes of the watching soldiers followed him, still expressing pleasure mixed, here and there, with grudging admiration.

"About time someone made that little bastard eat dirt!" a voice called with feeling.

"Look out!"

The strident warning could only be meant for Cuchillo. And the Apache would be attacked from only one quarter. He whirled and drew the golden knife. The stories he had heard of Bill Neat were true. The small, aging man did not just talk tough. He was tough. A reaction to pain was etched deeply into his rodent-like face, but he was able to overcome his agony as he sought immediate revenge. He had rolled over on to his belly again, raised himself on to his hands and knees, then lunged toward the Remington. The distance he had to cover was not great, and his right hand was curled, fingers hooked to scoop up the gun, when Cuchillo released the knife.

Just as when, a few moments earlier, the Apache had made a conscious decision not to kill Neat, so he made a similar choice. He did not want trouble of any kind. But trouble had come to him, and all he could do was try to minimize it. It would have been easy to thud the knife into Neat's heart. For a man of Cuchillo's skill, it was just as easy to direct the weapon into a less vital target.

The blade, hurled with tremendous force, bit into the center of Neat's palm just as the hand cupped to take a grip around the gun butt. It went deep into the hand and emerged at the back in a fine spray of blood. Only the jeweled hilt halted its flesh-tearing drive, but the power of the throw kept the knife moving. As Neat screamed at the new agony, his arm was flung to the side. The point of the knife dug into the wood of the store front and remained there, pinning the hand. Beads of crimson oozed from the entry and exit wounds and dropped to the ground.

Cuchillo had not confined his second counter-attack to the knife throw. Neat had already proved he did not submit easily and he had one good hand with which to reach for the gun. So Cuchillo lunged in the wake of the knife, and he kicked the Remington clear of the man on the ground before the initial wave of agony had washed from Neat's mind. There was fear in the rat-like eyes as they looked up at the tall Apache. Then he looked beyond Cuchillo, raking his gaze over the faces of the watching soldiers. His voice was low, but not from pain.

"Kill me, you stinkin' savage!" he said, taunting and pleading at the same time. "I'd rather be dead than have these bastards spread it around what a lousy Injun done to me."

Cuchillo stooped and the night air seemed to be vibrating with massed excitement and anticipation. "Another time and another place, White Eyes," he said softly. Then he rested a moccasined foot on Neat's wrist, grasped the handle of the knife, and jerked it clear of wood and flesh.

Neat screamed.

Cuchillo stayed bent, to wipe the blood from the blade on Neat's shirt. Then he straightened and thrust the knife into the waistband of his leggings. Neat raised his injured hand to his mouth and began to suck at the spilling blood. Now his eyes held only hatred and Cuchillo turned away from the familiar expression.

"Help me, gal!" Neat snarled.

"Yeah, do that!" the bearded sergeant called, his tone light. "Your Pa sure looks like he could use a hand."

CHAPTER FIVE

The three Mohave scouts were afraid of Cuchillo. He could not see them in the darkness of the spartanly furnished room with its five bunks and single washbasin. And they did not speak to him. But he could sense it as he lay stretched out on one of the two bunks which had no gear stowed beneath them. The Mohaves sat on their bunks, noisily eating, finishing the meal which the fight with Neat had interrupted. There was a natural enmity between Mohaves and Apaches. A lone Indian was distrusted by others of his race as much as by the White Eyes. And they had seen this lone Apache exhibit his strength and skill. Cuchillo understood their fear but did not feel moved to set their minds at rest.

For that would have involved talk and he was not yet ready for this. Perhaps later he would be forced to talk with the Mohaves, and the soldiers, in order to learn what he wanted to know about Pinner. But, for the present, he was content to let events take their course. Despite last night's rest and the food and water he had been allowed to have since meeting with the horsesoldiers, the grueling effects of heat exposure and being hunted by the band of Apaches were still with him. He knew this because of the weakness he felt after the fight with Neat. As he lay on the bunk in the darkness, he felt like an old man, many years progressed from a fit and strong Apache warrior able to meet confidently with a bitter and cunning enemy.

As he hovered on the fringe of sleep, he was aware that the return to full strength was the first priority. While he recovered, he would listen rather than question. Only if this strategy did not provide him with information about the whereabouts of Pinner would he make direct inquiries. But his questions would have to be discreetly phrased. Many eyes had seen his golden knife. Many ears must have heard the story of the bitter feud between an army captain and a lone Apache. It was probable that mention of such a unique weapon was often made in the telling of the story.

Aware of the danger attendant on his decision to take a job as army scout, Cuchillo slid into sleep: his tired mind ignoring the discontented rumblings of an empty stomach.

By degrees, the quiet fort became even quieter as the bulk of its manpower followed the Apache into sleep. The guard on the walkways and on the gate was changed. In the rear of the stable eight men got together and started two games of poker. At two o'clock, after the games were finished, a lone rider approached the fort, was challenged, and admitted. He was a corporal from the Department of New Mexico headquarters at Fort Marcy, Santa Fe. Colonel Zentner was roused from his bed to open the sealed dispatch brought by the messenger, and Wylie's commanding officer had the other officers wakened and gathered them in his office.

All this happened with the minimum of noise and little fuss. Those men whose rest was disturbed by the late night comings and goings quickly dropped off to sleep again. Although isolated, Wylie was strategically placed in the chain of forts and posts straddling Apacheria and few days or nights passed without messengers arriving from department headquarters. Mostly such visits entailed officer business. If the men were needed, they would be roused by more obtrusive sounds than those of footfalls and opening and closing doors.

Bill Neat was wide awake even before the messenger from Marcy cantered in through the gate. His stomach hurt bad from the head butt and his hand, cleaned and bandaged by Mary, hurt even worse. But, even had there been no physical pain, Neat knew he would have found sleep hard to come by. For his mind was broiling in a turmoil of bitter thoughts. A stinking savage had got the better of him, which was bad enough. Even worse, his humiliation had been enacted in front of almost every man on the fort. Living with this was not going to be easy. It was also going to make it difficult to keep the frigging noncoms and enlisted men from sniffing around his daughter.

Neat got out of his bed in the room behind the store, dressed painfully, and went outside for a walk and a smoke. His mind continued to create anxious new thoughts. Mary had it in her stupid head that she wanted to tie herself up with an Apache. He had managed to weaken her resolve on this but, in so doing, had invited a new problem. Mary was a woman with the normal physical needs: constantly surrounded with the opportunity to satisfy her desires.

He was pacing angrily up and down behind the company command office when the messenger came into Fort Wylie. The incident with the Mohave had been the first overt sign that Mary was prepared to lower her sights. If she couldn't get herself an Apache brave, then any Indian would do. But the Mohave had got his— in no way from the girl! Since then, Neat had often seen her give the come-on to certain soldiers around the fort and he had been encouraged by this. Because Mary was past ready for a man, she no longer made a distinction between Indian and white. But, knowing of Neat's ambitions for his daughter and recalling vividly what had happened to the Mohave scout, no man was willing to risk responding to Mary's blatant invitations.

Now though?

An orderly was sent to rouse the junior officers and they hurried to attend the late-night meeting in Zentner's office. Neat's anger rose as he continued to pace. Now that a filthy savage had hurt and humiliated him every man who had ever seen that come-hither look in Mary's eyes might well decide he could risk a response.

Neat was pulled up sharply in his pacing as a shaft of yellow light fell across his path. It came from a window at the rear of Zentner's office as the blind was raised to allow the window to be opened. Tobacco smoke drifted out through the window, blue in the yellow lamp light, and the blind was not pulled down again.

"Right, gentlemen," the familiar voice of the colonel announced in a businesslike tone. "I have called this briefing to discuss the contents of a dispatch I have just received from Santa Fe."

There were the sounds of chair springs and the scrape of boot leather on floorboards as the officers made themselves more comfortable. Neat didn't give a damn for any man inside the office. Four of the six officers were married and the two who were single—Lieutenant Ramsey and Lieutenant Secker—had no money beyond their army pay. Nor had he any interest in eavesdropping on the briefing session, until the colonel said something which caused him to halt his swing away from the open window.

"In short, the dispatch orders me to send a supply train to Fort Ryan because of a threatened uprising in that area."

Fort Ryan were the key words which opened up Neat's keen interest. He pressed himself tight against the wall and inched sideways until he was just outside the shaft of lamplight.

"So we were right in guessing our bunch of Apaches weren't the only ones turning hostile, sir?" Captain Pike said.

"Quite so," the colonel confirmed. "Intelligence reports indicate that *rancherias* throughout the Dragoon range are on the verge of erupting." There was a riffling of papers as Zentner checked over the recently delivered dispatch. "It looks like whites are at the root of the trouble. A dozen men—a mixture of Californians and Mexicans— are running liquor and guns on to the *rancherias*." He cleared his throat. "Maybe only ten of them now, since our troublemakers slaughtered their suppliers."

"No more trouble around here, sir?" Ramsey asked.

"It doesn't seem so, lieutenant. As you

© Lorillard 1975

C'mon

Come for the filter.

You'll stay for the taste.

19 mg. "tar," 1.2 mg. nicotine av. per cigarette, FTC Report Apr. '75.

Warning: The Surgeon General Has Determined That Cigarette Smoking Is Dangerous to Your Health.

© Lorillard 1975

I'd heard enough to make me decide one of two things: quit or smoke True.

I smoke True.
The low tar, low nicotine cigarette.
Think about it.

King Regular: 11 mg. "tar", 0.6 mg. nicotine,
King Menthol: 12 mg. "tar", 0.7 mg. nicotine, 100's
Regular: 13 mg. "tar", 0.7 mg. nicotine, 100's Menthol: 13 mg.
"tar", 0.8 mg. nicotine, av. per cigarette, FTC Report April '75.

Warning: The Surgeon General Has Determined
That Cigarette Smoking Is Dangerous to Your Health.

gentlemen know, the largest concentration of Apaches is to the south of here, with Fort Ryan slap bang in the middle of it. Reports indicate that if and when an uprising starts, Ryan will be the first objective. And Ryan is where the top brass at Santa Fe have decided to make a show of strength. A reinforcement column is being sent up there from Breckinridge. Our job is to get supplies of food and ammunition to the men already at Ryan and the company that's to join them."

At Fort Ryan there was a certain Captain Bradford Thorley who was the only son of one of the richest landowners in New England. As a man, the story went, he was no catch for any woman. But, as a provider, he was everything Neat had ever dreamed for his daughter.

"Captain Pike will be in command of the supplies train," Zentner went on. "Lieutenant Ramsey will go along, too. You two gentlemen will detail fifty men for the escort party in addition to ten wagon drivers."

"That many, sir?" somebody asked.

"That many," Zentner said firmly. "A train will take three days to reach Fort Ryan from here. So far, the only Apache trouble has been in our area. But the situation is volatile, gentlemen. From Wylie to Ryan, it's Apache country all the way. The blowup could come at any moment and I don't want an underdefended train caught out in the open."

There was more talk in the office, as the details of the train's make-up were discussed. But Neat hardly listened. If he and Mary were able to join the train it would solve a lot of problems. At Ryan, he would be able to forget about his humiliation. Mary would not be regarded as easy pickings after he had made his views on the subject known. And perhaps there would be a chance to gain the interest of the rich Captain Thorley.

"How about Indian scouts, sir?" Ramsey asked, capturing Neat's attention again. "The three Mohaves we have left are pretty well untried."

"It's Lieutenant Secker's job to assign scouts, Ramsey, you know that," the Colonel pointed out.

"I'd just like to say for the record that the Apache knows his business," Ramsey insisted.

Neat became tense, the lines of his thin face rigid. Under no circumstances did he want the Apache along on the supplies train.

"He's a troublemaker," Secker put in. "He almost killed the saddler last night."

"What's that?" the colonel demanded.

"A fight about Bill Neat's daughter," Captain Pike supplied. "But Neat wasn't almost killed. I'd say the Indian showed great restraint."

"Well, I wouldn't trust him, sir," Secker argued. "He drew a knife against a white man. And what a knife, sir. Ivory handle and gold hilt encrusted with precious stones. Must have cost a fortune so he must have stolen—"

"What's that you say?" Zentner cut in.

The lieutenant repeated his description.

"What's the Apache's name?" the colonel wanted to know.

"Cuchillo Oro, sir," Ramsey answered.

"Pinner's Indian," the senior man muttered.

Although he was unable to see in through the window without the risk of making his presence known, Neat sensed the officers were as intrigued by Zentner's comment as was he.

"Beg pardon, sir?" somebody asked.

"There is a cavalry captain named Pinner," the colonel explained. "Not the kind of officer I would wish under my command. Totally intolerant of all Indians. He owned such a knife as the lieutenant just described. This Cuchillo Oro was accused of stealing it. Some say falsely accused, and knowing of Pinner I am inclined to give the Apache the benefit of the doubt. There was a great deal of bitterness and Pinner mutilated the Apache's right hand."

"It's the same Apache, sir," Ramsey allowed.

"Quite so. It did not end there. The Apache's wife and child were killed by Pinner and then an army fort was completely destroyed."

"Shall I arrest him, sir?" Secker asked urgently.

"No, you shall not!" Zentner replied firmly. "No military order has been issued against the

Apache named Cuchillo Oro. It is a personal matter between this Captain Pinner and the Apache." He sighed. "As I have said, Lieutenant Secker, it is part of your duties to assign scouts. But, in making a decision with regard to the Indian who will go with tomorrow's train, there is something you should bear in mind. The reinforcement column en route from Breckinridge to Ryan is under the command of Captain Cyrus L. Pinner."

Neat underwent a radical change of mind concerning the Apache's presence on the train. He had heard enough and there was a crafty grin on his face as he withdrew from beside the open window. He felt good for the first time since seeing the tall Apache ride in through the gates at the head of the returning column. He was even able to ignore his injuries as he returned to his store. And he was just a little anxious—rather than troubled—as he stood in the doorway, waiting for the briefing session to break up.

When it did, and the officers filed out of the commander's office, he had no trouble in capturing the attention of Lieutenant Secker. Officers were the same as the men. They could never walk past the saddler's store without glancing toward it, ever hopeful of catching a glimpse of the only woman for miles around.

"Lieutenant Secker," he called. "About that new saddle."

Secker—short, overweight, and with a bad complexion under a head of thinning red hair—veered away from the direction he had been headed and crossed to where Neat stood, smiling at him.

"What new saddle?" he demanded.

"An excuse," Neat whispered, ushering him across the threshold. "Come inside. I have a proposition that might interest you."

The Lieutenant, who was forty years old and resigned to the fact that he would never be promoted beyond his present rank, complied with the request. "Proposition about what?" he asked, matching his voice to the low tone used by Neat. He sat down on a stack of leather as Neat closed the door.

"Couldn't sleep," Neat said. "On account of feelin' bad after that run-in with the savage."

"So?" Secker was both intrigued and suspicious. He could hear the regular breathing of the woman sleeping in one of the two back rooms.

"Was walkin' out back of the admin buildin' and I gotta admit I overheard some of what was said in there. Not on purpose, you understand—"

"Just be glad that what you heard wasn't classified, Neat!" Secker snapped.

"Hold on, Lieutenant," Neat said quickly. "Wait 'til you hear what I gotta say before you get steamed up."

93

Secker did listen, having to strain his hearing to pick up the quietly spoken words. It was almost pitch black inside the store and he was unable to see Neat's ratty face. Just the slight form of the man. And Secker was glad of the darkness, for it also meant that Neat was unable to see him as more than a silhouette, a lighter shadow against darker ones. For a whole gamut of expressions flicked across his features and some of these might have put off Neat from continuing. And, when Neat got to the point of the reward for what he was requesting, Secker could hardly contain himself. But he went through the motions of debating his decision, asking questions, and greeting the replies with long, apparently thoughtful, pauses.

Then: "Okay, Mr. Neat. You got yourself a deal. But how will your daughter—"

"My gal will do whatever I damn well tell her to do!" the saddler growled. "But I want your word you'll send the new Injun as scout for the train tomorrow."

"You got it," Secker assured.

"You ready now?"

"What do you think?"

"I reckon you're ready," Neat allowed, and there was a tone of regret in his voice for the first time since he had invited Lieutenant Secker into his store. "I'll go tell her."

He moved quickly, as if afraid he would

change his mind if he allowed himself time to think about what was to happen.

"I'll wait for you to give me the word it's okay," the officer called, his voice thick with excited anticipation.

"It'll be okay," Neat responded, and went out through the door at the rear of the store and into the living quarters.

Secker crept closer to the door, straining his ears to pick up what was said. But the voices were too low: just an urgent mumbling, the father's demands barely distinguishable from the daughter's protest. Then there was a sharp crack of flesh against flesh, a strangled cry of pain, and a sentence that was clearly audible.

"You been hangin' out the sign long enough, gal—now you got a customer, is all."

His footfalls sounded angry. Secker backed away from the doorway, but Neat banged in to him anyway. The slightly built saddler jerked a thumb over his shoulder and gave a curt nod. The Lieutenant almost tripped over his own feet in his haste to get to Mary's room, his anticipation heightened by the fact that she would be submitting to him under duress. He had his coat and hat off and was beginning to unbutton his shirt as he entered the room.

He was halted abruptly by the sight that greeted him, as a match flared and ignited the wick of a lamp. Mary Neat had not waited inactively after her father had left her. She had thrown off the covers, shrugged out of her night dress, and prepared the lamp for lighting. Now she spread her naked body out on the bed, her legs splayed to gape her hirsute sex as her hands cupped her trim breasts, fingers and thumbs toying wantonly with the dark nipples.

"Does it shock you, White Eyes horse-soldier?" she asked, the expression of her eyes and mouth backing up the wanton pose. "My father treats me as a whore, so I am acting like such a cheap woman."

Secker had been almost ready just thinking about taking the woman. Seeing her, naked and promiscuous, brought him to the very brink of spending himself before he could touch her. "Some shocks are good for a man, Miss Mary," he growled, and back-heeled the door to close it.

His lustful eyes and the way that he tore at his clothes to free them from his body, set a grip of terror on to the woman. The brazen display of sexuality had been a ploy, by which she had hoped to alienate Secker. But it was obvious that it had had the opposite effect. Now, she curled up into a ball and dragged a blanket over her nakedness.

"Please?" she begged, as the man removed the final article of clothing to leave him as naked as she was. "I've never—"

"Makes it even better," he said, approaching the bed, hooking a hand over the top of the blanket and ripping it off her.

The woman stared at the ramrod stiffness of him and her terror increased. It seemed impossible that she could accommodate such a male monstrosity. But nothing was so terrible as her father's anger and she knew she dare not scream.

But Secker did not know this, and the hand that had stripped the blanket from her body now clamped over her mouth. Her dark eyes expressed tacit pleas, but he was not looking at her face. His gaze swept back and forth over her body, and then his free hand began to explore what his eyes could see. Her firm flesh was ice cold to the touch of his fingers as they trailed over the mounds of her breasts, across her stomach, and down the slender lengths of her thighs.

His touch was gentle at first, but then the hand became a claw and he used it as a weapon, applying all his strength to force her to spread herself full length along the bed. Mary resisted, but did not struggle and she was no match for Secker's insistent strength. While his right hand continued to be clamped over her mouth, his left clawed across her breast as he kneeled on the bed and then lowered his body on top of hers. He was soaked with the sweat of desire but the rigid center of his want was hotter than any other surface of his body. The pressure of his thighs forced Mary to part hers and his hand left her breast to grasp himself.

She was dry. He guided himself against her and into her, cursing as he struggled to hold back his climax until he had gained entry. Her scream was silent, forcing hot breath against the palm of his hand. It was caused by pain rather than terror. The way became greased by the warm moisture of blood.

Pain was gone and pleasure vibrated through every fiber of the woman's body. She hated the sweating, thrusting man who had violated her: detested herself for allowing the coupling. But, despite this, her arms folded around his back and her legs parted wider and then she locked her feet behind his legs. Her pores oozed sweat to mix with his and their flesh made small sucking sounds as it was ground together. She began to moan and he freed her mouth to allow exit to her delight. She thrust as hard against him as he did into her. He spent himself and she continued to writhe beneath him, demanding her own satisfaction before he could shrivel. But he was exhausted and rolled off her. As her grip was broken on him, she grasped one of his hands in both of hers and forced it down to her moist crotch.

Her moans rose to the point of screams and he covered her mouth again. Her body arched as she forced his fingers inside her. Mary Neat achieved orgasm and returned to reality. She experienced a degree of hatred only possible to someone with Apache blood in her veins. And, as she looked at herself and at Secker in the low level of lamplight, she hated herself more than anything or anybody in the world.

"Pretty good, uh?" the ugly lieutenant asked, grinning as he used a blanket to wipe himself. "You got a lot to catch up on, since you been missing out so long."

"Get out!" Mary snarled at him, dragging the blanket across her body again. "I never want to see you again."

Secker held the smile in place as he dressed. He did not reply until he was fully attired. Then he crossed to the side of the bed, forcing her to look at him. "All you made was a down payment, Miss Mary," he rasped. "And you can't deny you didn't enjoy making it. So you got something to look forward to tomorrow night."

"No!"

It was not the woman who made the protest. The door had swung open and Bill Neat stood there, on the fringe of the lamplight. "She's goin' on the supplies train." His thin face expressed a mixture of anger and disgust. "That was the deal. You assign the Apache to the train and you get to have Mary. Just the once."

Secker was supremely confident. He shrugged as he turned from the bed to head for the door. "Okay, if you want to stick to that deal. But if Miss Mary heads out of Wylie in the morning, I'll make sure every man on the train knows how much she likes what everyone of them can give her."

Neat stepped out of Secker's way and the lieutenant crossed the threshold. His footfalls were heavy on the floor of the store. He slammed the front door hard behind him.

"Why didn't you kill him?" Mary snarled at her father. "I'd have backed you. We could have said he raped me."

Her father was sagging against the door frame, white-faced and looking smaller than he was. He shook his head. "What decent man would want to marry a woman that's been raped?" he asked.

"Dear God!" Mary gasped. "What man would want one who lost her virginity in a deal made by her father?"

Neat pulled himself erect and stared grimly at his daughter, who stared back with utter contempt. "Don't you worry none about that, my gal," he rasped. "I'll kill that welshin' bastard at the right time and ain't no one'll know what he done to you."

"I'll know, Pa," she muttered. "I'll know, and I'll know it was really you done it to me."

He moved quickly to the side of the bed and she tried to cower away from him. But he was too quick for her. His good hand lashed her viciously across the cheek.

"You can't lose your shame by beating me!" she challenged.

He nodded. "I'm ashamed, gal," he retorted. "But not of myself. I'm ashamed of you. That bastard wasn't tellin' no lie. I heard for myself. You enjoyed him."

Lieutenant Secker was still relishing his own enjoyment as he entered the scouts' quarters, jerking awake Cuchillo and the three Mohaves as the door banged back against the wall.

"Apache!" he rasped.

"You want me?" Cuchillo asked.

"I don't want nothing to do with you, Injun," Secker snapped. "But then I ain't going out on the supplies train that will leave the fort at seven o'clock in the morning. You are, as scout. Be ready to leave."

"Why him?" one of the Mohaves asked sullenly. "We senior scouts now Hunter Man dead." He spat. "Why Apache go? He just come?"

Secker vented a harsh laugh as he swung toward the door. "His coming had nothing to do with it," he growled.

CHAPTER SIX

The sun was well clear of the eastern horizon and radiating a promise of high heat to come as the ten-wagon supply train rolled out of the gates of Fort Wylie the next morning. Like the men detailed to drive and escort the wagons, Cuchillo was roused two hours before the seven o'clock departure time. He was given breakfast and was then allowed to study a chart showing the proposed route between Wylie and Ryan. Both Captain Pike and Lieutenant Ramsey watched him closely as he examined the chart. Ramsey had no doubts about the Apache's ability to do a good job of scouting. And Pike was quickly convinced that the lieutenant's trust was well placed. It was obvious, both from the questions he asked and the suggestions he made, that Cuchillo Oro understood the chart and appreciated the problems of traveling the route it showed.

He was given an outline of the reason for the train and only one fact was withheld from him—the name of the officer commanding the column of reinforcements headed for Fort Ryan. The decision to make this omission was reached jointly by the lieutenant and the captain. Taking the train south might be easy or it might be dogged by trouble. If the latter proved to be the case, it would not be helped by having a scout whose mind was concerned with other things.

So it was that Cuchillo, riding immediately behind Pike and Ramsey at the head of the train, left Fort Wylie in total ignorance that at the end of the trail he could well complete his deadly mission.

By the time of the departure, with freshly shaven men astride rested horses, escorting heavily laden wagons pulled by strong teams, the daily routine business of the fort had commenced. And many pairs of eyes watched the train pull out and swing into a hundred and eighty degree turn to head south. There were too many watchers, in fact, for certain individuals to be missed. Unless one happened to be looking for familiar faces. And no one was. So the absence of Lieutenant Secker, Bill Neat, and his daughter was not noticed by anybody on the train. For every mind was concerned with the prospect of three days crossing difficult terrain—terrain which at any time could become stained with the blood of an Indian uprising.

And, as the morning wore on, the sun getting hotter as it climbed higher, nobody was fooled into a false sense of security by the lack of trouble. Progress was slow and, therefore, Fort Wylie was always just a short, fast ride away. One band of drunken, kill-crazy Indians had already made the mistake of causing trouble in the vicinity of the fort. There had been no survivors from the bloodbath that had punished the mistake, but there didn't have to be. The Indians had a highly developed telegraph system of their own, which needed no talking wires on high poles. It was a message-carrying system that was both sophisticated and primitive, seeming sometimes to depend upon unexplained magic. But, however it worked, it was efficient. And there was no doubt that by now every Apache within the territorial jurisdiction of Fort Wylie knew of the massacre in the canyon.

Despite the sound reasoning that precluded trouble over the first leg of the trek, Cuchillo was sent ahead to scout the country. But he was not looking only for Indian signs. The charted route from Wylie to Ryan provided simply an indication of the way to take. There was not a well-used trail to follow, for traffic between the two strategically placed army posts was light to the point of almost nonexistence. Wind and flash storms could have altered the basic structure of some parts of the country since the last journey was made—though perhaps not enough to interfere with the movement of riders. But a rock fall or a newly opened gorge could well cause a train of heavily laden wagons to make a wide detour.

But the way was clear all through the morning. Cuchillo rejoined the train at the halt for the noon meal, then cantered ahead again, to hold a position a half-mile in front of the two soldiers riding at point.

He found Lieutenant Secker midway through the afternoon. He smelled the man first, although he was not sure it was a man. The strong, sickly sweet odour of something long dead might have come from a slaughtered animal. The fact of death caused the Apache to draw his Colt as he slowed his gelding and then slid from the saddle to lead the horse forward. He was at the base of a hill, with the train out of sight behind the high ground. A broad sweep of relatively flat country lay ahead, but twenty yards away, on the left, there was a stunted outcrop of rock. It was from beyond this that the stench emanated.

Cuchillo rounded the pitted, sun-bleached rock with the cocked revolver thrust out in front of him. He saw the body of Secker and holstered the gun as he released the reins of the gelding. The well-schooled horse stood stock-still, head low so that the reins touched the ground. The body was spread-angled, ten feet from where Cuchillo stood. He was naked and his wrists and ankles were lashed by leather thongs to stakes driven into the ground. The sun shafted down upon his unprotected flesh, but its harsh heat had not contributed to the Lieutenant's suffering. It was a knife that had tortured the man. First the fingers of each hand had been hacked off below the lowest joint. Then he had been gelded. Next scalped. Finally, an enormous hole had been carved into his chest and the heart had been ripped from the body.

Cuchillo guessed at the order of the mutilation, basing it upon the sequence that would cause Lieutenant Secker the most agony. The displaced pieces of the man's anatomy were piled in a heap a few inches from his head. His torn and tattered clothing were placed a few feet away.

"You found somethin', Injun?" a voice called.

Cuchillo looked back up the hill and saw that the two men riding point had crested the rise and reined in their horses. They had their Spencer rifles out of the saddleboots. He beckoned to them and they came at the gallop, keeping their rifles out. They stayed mounted after their horses had skidded to a halt. The Apache saw their faces pale. The younger man swayed in his saddle, but held his seat as he vomited. The other man aimed his Spencer at Cuchillo.

"That's Lieutenant Secker!" he croaked, failing to get any authority into his tone.

Cuchillo nodded. "Man who send me on this job. But I want job. Anyway, he been dead many hours."

This fact was easy to detect with nose and eyes. The smell was overpowering. The blood was crusted hard and deep black. The man booted his Spencer and gave a nod of his own as Pike and Ramsey led the head of the column over the rise.

"You're right," he allowed as the young soldier emptied his stomach. "But it sure looks like the work of Injuns. What with the scalping and that."

"Looks like," Cuchillo agreed. "But Indian with stolen boots and horse. Both well-shod."

He pointed to the foot and hoofprints in the dust.

Seeing the soldier being sick while the second point rider and Cuchillo looked behind the stunted outcrop of rock, the two officers detailed six of the escort and rode down the slope leaving the column in a stall. The eight newcomers showed wan-faced grimaces as they saw the remains of Lieutenant Secker.

Pike and Ramsey were given a fast outline of Cuchillo's contentions about the murder, studied the evidence themselves, and agreed with the inconclusiveness. Secker might have been killed by an Indian or a white man several hours previously.

"But what the hell was he doing out here, sir?" a corporal asked.

"How the hell would I know, soldier?" the solidly built, dour-faced Pike snapped. "You ride back to Wylie and report the matter to Colonel Zentner." He stabbed a gloved finger at two enlisted men. "You and you, dig a grave and bury the officer. Catch up with the train after the job's done."

He stood in his stirrups and signaled for the train to start down the slope. The corporal set off at a gallop, backtracking on the day's trek. The two men detailed to grave-digging dismounted and waited to lift shovels off the lead wagon. A driver and an escort were sick to their stomachs when they saw the mutilated corpse.

"You got any more ideas about what happened, mister?" Ramsey asked as he and Pike flanked Cuchillo at the head of the rolling train again. The open terrain ahead made it unnecessary for forward scouting.

"I think he was brought from fort," the Apache replied.

"Against his will?" This from the grim-faced Pike.

Cuchillo held up a pair of fingers of his good hand. "Two horses ridden to place where horse-soldier officer killed. One, only lightly burdened, stop only moment and ridden south again. Second horse carry heavy weight to rock. After killing, ridden south like other horse. Make tracks not so deep as before."

He pointed at the ground ahead, which plainly showed signs of hoofprints.

"You saying two riders left Wylie last night, one carrying Lieutenant Secker along with him?" This from Ramsey.

"I say looks like," Cuchillo replied flatly.

"How could that be?" the lieutenant demanded. "Without the guards being alerted?"

Cuchillo shrugged. "I had no reason to look for sign at fort."

"It could be, Lieutenant," Pike mused sourly. "You haven't been at Wylie long."

"A month, sir."

"You haven't heard about the tunnel."

"Tunnel, Captain?"

A nod. "Sure. A piece of inspired design which it hasn't ever been necessary to use. The entrance is inside the stables. Cuts down into the hill and comes out behind a heap of rocks on the east incline. If ever Wylie was under siege, every man, animal, and piece of equipment could be got out from behind the walls by using the tunnel. It would take time, but it could be done. Two horses and three men could be out and clear in less than ten minutes."

"It isn't guarded, sir?"

"Against what?" Pike asked.

The question put an end to the conversation. The day began to cool as afternoon faded toward evening. The two grave-diggers galloped up to rejoin the train and the slopes of higher ground showed ahead. Men were detailed to ride at point and Cuchillo was sent to scout the high country. The sun was down and a cool twilight lay across the Dragoons when he saw the farm.

He spotted it as he emerged from a low-sided canyon, plenty wide enough to allow access to the wagons. It wasn't good farming country and the buildings reflected the poor rewards from the parched fields of dead and dying crops. There was a small shack and a larger combined barn and stable. They were crudely built of used timber and adobe. A buckboard was parked between them.

The small homestead stood in the center of a dish of land between towering cliffs which provided shelter from every kind of weather save harsh sun. An arroyo cut across from an aperture at the base of the eastern cliff, to show that at infrequent intervals the farm would have a supply of water.

Cuchillo remained at the mouth of the canyon, narrowed-eyes surveying the marks of man on nature. There was no smell of death in the quiet air, but he sensed that something was wrong. No light showed at the windows of the shack, and no smoke rose from the chimney. But the quality of the place which the Apache sensed was not of abandonment. Rather, he had the strong impression that the farm was occupied.

He heard the sound of horses approaching from behind him, but did not turn around as the point riders closed in on him.

"You figure trouble?" a man asked, his voice lowered to a whisper. By instinct of logic, he was aware that sound would carry between the natural funnel of the towering cliff faces.

"This place not shown on army chart," Cuchillo answered.

The other man spat. "Ain't nothin' strange about that, feller. Indian like you oughta know that. Crazy folks from back east are always comin' out here to try their hands at dirt farmin' in all the wrong places."

"Sure looks like it ain't been here long," the other soldier commented, having to strain his eyes to peer through the failing light.

"What's it matter, anyway?" his companion asked. "Ain't exactly big enough to hide a thousand hostiles. Let's check it out."

He heeled his horse forward. The other man shot a sidelong glance at Cuchillo, then nodded for him to go ahead. "You're gettin' paid to scout," he pointed out.

Cuchillo acknowledged the truth of this with a nod of his own, and urged the gelding forward. He rode with a hand draped over the butt of the holstered Colt. As they left the mouth of the canyon, they could hear the sound of the train rolling along behind them.

Out in the open, the man who had made the decision to approach the farm, held back until the others caught up with him. He had sensed there was something to fear about the farmstead and there was a suspicious look on his face as he unbooted his rifle.

"You got the feelin', too, Hyram?" the other soldier asked, drawing his own Spencer.

Hyram spat. "Yeah, John. I got an itch in the ass and that's a sign that never fails. Maybe there ain't no thousand hostiles in that place. But there could be enough of 'em to blast you, me, and the Injun into hell."

It was a hundred yards from the mouth of the canyon to the outer edge of a corn field. They covered this distance in line abreast, then started across the field, the withering crops being trampled under the slow-moving hooves of their horses. The house was fifty yards away. They were halfway to it when a rifle shot sounded.

All three riders toppled themselves from their saddles, thudding into the insecure cover of the stunted crop. They heard the smash of shattered glass and then the hiss of the bullet. Cuchillo's revolver and the Spencers of the two soldiers cracked out in unison. More glass was shattered as all three bullets crashed into the shards remaining in the window to one side of the shack's door. Hoofbeats vibrated in the air as men at the head of the wagon train galloped their horses toward the sounds of the gunfire.

A woman's scream froze the two soldiers and the Apache in the act of sending a second volley of shots toward the shack.

"What the hell?" John exclaimed.

"Got a hostage," Hyram suggested.

"You men?" the recognizable voice of Captain Pike yelled. "What's happening?"

But neither of the soldiers had time to reply.

"Thank God!" a woman shrieked from the shack. "I thought it was them come back!"

The door of the shack was flung wide and the woman half-ran, half-stumbled across the threshold. But nobody had to see her to know who she was. They had all recognized the voice of Mary Neat. She still had a rifle in her hands, but she threw it down as if it revolted her as Cuchillo and the two soldiers rose from out of the corn and Pike led a bunch of a dozen men out of the canyon mouth.

"She took a shot at us, sir," John reported.

The woman, wearing the same dress as last night, but with a cape over her shoulders and a bonnet hanging down her back, waited until all the men had halted their horses in a half-circle around the front of the shack.

"I didn't know who it was," she pleaded. "I thought it was them come back again."

Genuine terror was still apparent in her eyes, beneath the relief that had established a firmer hold on her emotions.

"Who, Miss Mary?" Pike asked, with no trace of sympathy in his voice.

"The ones who did this."

She stepped aside from the doorway and nodded towards the interior of the shack. Pike dismounted and strode toward the doorway. The woman swept her gaze across the face of every man, seeking in vain for a glimmer of compassion. But every soldier assigned to the wagon train had seen the butchered body of Secker— and Cuchillo's theory about the murder had reached all ears. Mary Neat saw only suspicion in their hard-eyed responses to her pleading.

"White men and Apaches!" she cried. "At least twenty, I think. I could not see properly just now. I see just the shadows of three men coming. I did not see they were in soldiers' uniforms."

A match struck inside the shack and Pike gasped, then vented a low obscenity. "Lieutenant! Scout! Come in here!"

The dim light of the match moved, then was expanded as it was touched to a lamp wick. The designated men slid from their saddles and advanced on the doorway. Ramsey beckoned the Apache in ahead of him.

"Oh, sweet Jes . . ." Ramsey started to say as he peered over Cuchillo's shoulder.

"Hostilities have started!" Pike snapped across the voice of the junior officer.

Cuchillo's eyes, which had seen so much brutality and suffering, surveyed the interior of the shack without betraying his reaction to the scene. The building was as crude inside as it had appeared from the exterior. It was comprised of a single room, with the kitchen and parlor partitioned off from the sleeping quarters by two blankets hung over a length of rope. There was a double and a single bed on one side of the blankets. On the other was a stove, a bureau made of crates, a table, and three chairs. The walls and ceiling were of untreated timber and adobe. The floor was hard-packed dirt. The natural color scheme was gray and black. Crimson was a recent addition.

The blood of a middle-aged couple and a young girl of about sixteen had been spilled. They were recognizable from their severed heads, which had been stood, like ornaments, along a shelf which had once held crockery. The rest of the trio's remains were almost completely destroyed—reduced to bones piled on a broad patch of animal fat in front of the stove.

The atrocity had not been committed very long ago. The smell of boiling flesh had left the shack but the three heads were only now beginning to give off the first taint of decomposition.

"It was awful," Mary said.

The men inside looked toward the bullet-shattered window. The woman's face showed there, along with those of several soldiers. Other soldiers were at the second window, and some stood in the doorway. Perhaps the earlier sight of Lieutenant Secker had hardened the men, or maybe the fact that the farming family were strangers lessened the impact of the horror: whichever, the watchers were able to contain their shock.

"I got here at noon," the woman continued. "The people here said I could share a meal with them. I was attending to my horse in the barn when the men came."

"How many Indians, how many whites?" Pike demanded.

"Ten White Eyes," she replied dully, and eyed Cuchillo anxiously. "At least as many Apaches. The farmer and his wife and daughter —they tried to be friendly. They were taken into the house. I heard screams. Laughter. Two Apaches came to the barn, but I hid under the hay. They took my horse and the team for the wagon. The fire was already lit for cooking the meal. I couldn't see what was happening in here. But I could hear the men laughing and shouting. They were drinking. Sometimes they came outside to relieve themselves. Always they had bottles. Then I smelled what was in the smoke from the chimney. I was sick to my

116

stomach. It was only because they made so much noise they did not hear me."

"How long they been gone?" Pike asked grimly.

"Not long. An hour, no more. I came to the house afterward and saw it like this. I fainted. When I awake, I hear men coming, then see them. I feel sure I am in danger. That is when I shot the gun at them."

Pike glanced around the room again, avoiding the grisly heads atop the shelf. "Let's move the train out!" he said suddenly, striding to the door.

"Bury what's left of these people?" Ramsey asked, scurrying to get outside.

"No time!" the captain responded. "The Apaches have hit the warpath, that's for sure. We got to pull out all the stops to reach Fort Ryan."

Cuchillo left the shack ahead of Pike, who turned in the dorway and drew his revolver. The gun blasted a shot across the bloodstained room and shattered the lamp. Flaming oil sprayed over the blankets and set them alight.

"Fire's as good as burial," he said curtly, and hurried to mount up.

"You'll take me with you?" Mary begged, as all the men swung into their saddles.

"Sure you're coming with us," the captain retorted, beckoning for the train to start rolling out of the canyon toward the shack. "And you'd better have a good story to tell, Miss Mary. About what you're doing out here and about what happened to Lieutenant Secker."

The woman showed fear as dominant above relief now.

"You'll ride aboard the first wagon," Pike instructed. "And you'll be ready to give me a full explanation when we make camp—at the first suitable site the scout can find."

He glowered at Cuchillo as he finished speaking, and the Apache saw the bitter hatred in the captain's eyes. Pike was ignoring the possibility that a white man might have tortured and murdered Secker. He was also setting aside the fact that Mary Neat had seen both whites and Indians at the shack. Perhaps, even, he did not believe her. Whatever, there was the mark of Apache savagery on both crimes and he was tarring all Indians with the same brush. And Cuchillo was a full-blooded Apache while Mary was a half-breed. It was not a new experience for either of them to have to suffer a backlash of white hatred because of wrongs committed by others of their race.

In this instance, Cuchillo was more fortunate than the woman. While she was forced to ride among the soldiers, listening to their angry murmurings and feeling their hard-eyed stares upon her, he was able to galop off alone, riding far ahead of the column to scout out a safe haven for a camp.

118

He found such a place, at the center of a plateau, where the wagons could be drawn up into a defensive circle. He posted sentries that were able to see at least a half mile in all directions over open terrain. The campsite was five miles beyond the tiny farmstead, straddling the tracks left by the score of men who had attacked the couple and their daughter.

The cooks prepared a meal and those who could face food ate. Then, within the hearing of every man, Pike questioned Mary Neat about the events leading up to her presence at the farmstead. Her responses were slow at first, and her voice trembled with nervousness under the hard-eyed scrutiny of so many men. But then, as she met the impassive gaze of Cuchillo Oro, she gained in confidence. The Apache, seated on the ground with his back leaning against a wagon wheel, offered her no encouragement or compassion. But neither did he express tacit suspicion and hatred.

"I will tell exactly as it happened," she said abruptly, clutching the cape to her throat and cutting across one of Pike's questions. "As everyone here know, there is hate between my father and me."

She broke her gaze away from Cuchillo's eyes and raked a stare around the ring of faces, looking for affirmative gestures. None was forthcoming. She returned her concentration to Cuchillo and continued.

"This is true. When I hear that this train is going to Fort Ryan, I asked Lieutenant Secker if I can come aboard."

"Who told you about the train?" Pike demanded.

"Lieutenant Secker," she answered. "He comes to me last night as he has come on many other nights."

This produced a reaction from the men. A mumble of conversation sounded within the ring of wagons. The tone was a mixture of disbelief and surprise.

"Why'd he come to you?"

"Last night?"

"Any night!"

The woman's cheeks flushed, the colouring clear to see in the flickering firelight. She hung her head to stare at the ground now. "Can you not guess, Captain Pike?"

The officer made a sound of disgust. "I don't have to guess about your father's aims for you, lady," he snapped. "He wanted you to do better than Lieutenant Secker."

"My father is heavy sleeper," she answered, and now she directed her eyes constantly toward the ground just in front of her folded legs. "When he slept, Lieutenant Secker came to my room."

"Not last night, Captain," Ramsey said suddenly. "Don't you remember? After the meeting with the colonel broke up. Her father called Secker over to his store."

"Sure, Lieutenant," Pike allowed. "I recall that. What do you say, lady?"

"I know nothing of this," Mary answered at once. "I only know that Lieutenant Secker come to my room same way as always—through window I leave open. He come and . . . and . . . afterward, he tell me about train to take supplies to Fort Ryan. It is then I ask him if I can go to escape from my father. But he say no, because he not go on train and he wants me to stay near him.

"After he leaves, I get idea. I think I leave fort. Through tunnel so that guards not see me. I ride south for many miles and wait for train. I think then you allow me to ride on train to Fort Ryan—if I am too far away to be sent back. I not expect to be at farm when the men come to attack it."

She raised her head now, and swept her dark eyes around the ring of faces. In the fire light, they showed her suffering and they pleaded that her story should be accepted. Every man with the exception of Cuchillo continued to distrust her. The Apache brave did not alter his attitude of complete indifference.

"What do you think, lieutenant?" Pike asked, to end a long silence.

"Guess it could be true, sir," Ramsey allowed. "There certainly isn't any love lost between

Miss Mary and her father. But I don't understand her accepting Secker's attentions when she's always made it plain she wants an Apache."

"Apache braves are hard to find in an army fort!" the woman snapped. "And I was never allowed outside the gates." She pointed a shaking finger at Cuchillo. "He is the first to have entered Wylie since my father and I came there. And I am a fully grown woman!"

"Ain't no arguing against that," the bearded sergeant called from under a wagon. He punctuated the comment with a loud spit of tobacco juice.

A blaze of anger showed in the woman's dark eyes as she made yet another sweeping survey of the soldiers. "And why Lieutenant Secker?" she demanded. "Because he was the only one of you who had the courage to ignore my father's threats. That is the reason."

"Faint heart never did win no lady," the noncom growled. "Fair or dark."

"He didn't look like no winner back aways," somebody else called.

"For sure!" the sergeant allowed sourly.

The woman was confused by the exchange, and her eyes asked tacit questions of many faces, then settled their inquiry upon Pike.

"The lieutenant's dead," the captain supplied.

He watched closely, but was unable to tell

if the shock which entered Mary's eyes was genuine or false.

"Lone rider comin', sir!" one of the guards on the north side of the ring of wagons called.

There was the sound of many repeater actions being pumped. Then the beat of galloping hooves.

"It's okay, it's Corporal Welles!" a man shouted.

The corporal—the one who had been sent back to Wylie to report on the murder of Secker—rode through a gap between two wagons and dismounted. He looked long and hard at the woman, then remembered to salute Pike.

"Only one missin' now, sir," he said a little breathless after the galloping run-in on the wagon circle.

"What's that supposed to mean, man?" Pike demanded angrily.

"Sorry, sir. Colonel Zentner had a roll call made at the fort, sir. Only people not accounted for were Lieutenant Secker, Miss Mary, and the saddler, sir."

All attention swung back toward the woman.

"You sure your father never knew about Secker's visits to you, lady?" Pike asked.

She seemed about to give a fast reply, but held it back. The shock of hearing about Secker's death was still apparent in her eyes.

"I've never been sure of anything about my father," she answered at length.

Pike turned his attention to Cuchillo. "Those tracks back at where the murder happened? Any way of telling if the two riders were together or one was following the other at a distance?"

"No way," the Apache answered shortly.

"If my father left fort, he was not with me, I—" Mary began.

"Forget it, lady!" Pike cut her off. "We aren't equipped and we haven't got the time to hold a court of inquiry out here. We need rest to make an early start. Consider yourself under open arrest. Lieutenant Ramsey, I'm holding you responsible for her safekeeping."

"Yes, sir!" Ramsey acknowledged.

"Rest of you men not assigned guard duty, bed down."

The men dispersed from the group, to spread their blankets close to fires and beneath wagons. For awhile, low-voiced talk was exchanged.

"Imagine Lieutenant Secker gettin' to screw the breed dame," somebody said.

"You reckon her old man found out and wasted Secker?" another asked.

"Sure looks that way, seein' as how the Lieutenant's balls was cropped."

"Man, to think she give me the come-on one time! Sure am glad I didn't try slippin' it to her."

"You never did have any guts."

"Maybe not, but I still got my balls."

"Come on, you guys," a man groaned. "Quiet down and let's get some sleep. Have a heart."

"Still got one of them, too."

"And a couple of handfuls of fingers," a man rasped. "Now the inventory's completed, let's get some sleep."

"I just can't get the thought of Secker and the half-breed woman outta my mind."

"So keep 'em there for Christ sake! We just got through figurin' out you got what it takes to do something about it."

"Quiet you men!"

"Yeah, shuddup! Get a grip on yourself."

CHAPTER SEVEN

It was midafternoon of the next day when the supplies train cut on to a stageline trail that swung in from the northeast and ran south. On the chart, it was shown as the link between Silver City and Tombstone and it marked the end of the worst stretch of country the wagons had to cover. The trip, as far as the terrain was concerned, would be smooth from here on in, for the trail ran immediately past the gates of Fort Ryan.

But there was no guarantee about any other aspect of the long trek south. The trail showed the way to take, picking the line of least resistance through the central Dragoons. But the country to either side was more rugged than ever, providing countless sites from which to spring an ambush. Captain Pike pushed his points further ahead than before and doubled the strength of the outriders. Cuchillo scouted out of sight of the rolling wagons, beyond jagged ridges and around wide sweeps of trail curved around the higher peaks.

He had listened to the captain's warning to take extra care, but such an instruction had not been necessary. The Apache scout knew they were beyond the point of no return—closer to Fort Ryan than to Wylie. Thus, if an Indian attack was launched there was little chance of summoning help from Wylie. And it was unlikely the commander of Fort Ryan would be able to spare many men since he was expecting his own trouble with the hostile Indians. And the Apaches on the warpath must now be aware that the train, heavily laden with a valuable cargo of supplies, was enroute for Ryan. Put this all together, and it was past time for the column of wagons and escort to be hit.

But the stageline way station was not a good place to spring an attack.

Cuchillo saw it as he rode around the base of a hill: a single one-story building with a high water tower at the side. It looked peaceful and welcoming in the failing sunlight of later afternoon. But he did not make his assessment on a first impression. The way station stood at the center of a broad plateau with open ground stretched out on all sides. He halted the gelding and raised Lieutenant Ramsey's binoculars to his unblinking eyes. The powerful lenses greatly reduced the half mile distance to the building— and showed reassuring signs that all was well.

There was a stoop along the front of the building, facing west and catching the reddening rays from the sinking sun. Four White Eyes were on the stoop—two sprawled in rocking chairs and two squatting, their backs against the building wall. One man was smoking and another was whittling a length of wood. Cuchillo raked the glasses to the left, focusing them on the wide entrance to the stable at the side of the building. Despite the deep shade inside, the binoculars enabled him to count four horses tethered to a feed box. All of them were still saddled.

The way station looked safe enough, but Cuchillo did not risk a lone approach. Apaches all over the territory were rising up against the White Eyes and he was an Apache. True, he wore an army shirt, tunic, forage cap, and carried an army issue Colt and binoculars. But there was only his word that he had not stolen these from a horsesoldier he had killed. And, because of the Indian trouble, it was highly likely the men at the way station would not allow him close enough to exchange words.

So he waited in the deep shadows at the base of the hill until the point riders, then the two officers and lead wagon, caught up with him. Ramsey was given back his glasses and both he and Pike surveyed the way station.

"Where's the rest we started out with?" one

of the point riders asked the bearded sergeant who drove the lead wagon.

The noncom spat tobacco juice. "Second in line snapped its tongue."

"Looks okay," Pike commented.

"Yes, sir," Ramsey agreed.

The five horsemen and the wagon started out across the open ground. The approach was seen while the men were still some way off, but those on the building stoop showed little reaction to the appearance of the army. The smoking man arced his cigarette out into the open and the man who had been whittling put away his knife. They remained seated and squatting, even when the wagon and its escorting riders halted immediately opposite the station.

"Evening," Pike greeted brightly.

Like the others, he studied the civilians. The eldest—about fifty—had a completely bald head and a bushy mustache. The others were all in their early thirties. Every man had a thick growth of stubble on his jaw and cheeks and all their clothing was thickly covered with trail dust.

"It's a pretty good one," the bald-headed man allowed coldly.

"Seen any trace of Indians?"

"Just the one."

"Around here?" Pike demanded.

The whittling man had been making a wood

carving of a naked woman with out-of-proportion breasts. He pointed his handiwork at Cuchillo. "Reckon Art means him," he answered on behalf of the bald-headed man.

All four laughed.

Pike flushed. "A full-scale Indian war is no joking matter!" he snapped.

"Heard about that," Art drawled. "We was worried, but we ain't no more." He raked his smirking eyes over the travel-weary soldiers. "Seein' as how the brave soldier boys are around to protect us now."

He spat, arcing the globule of saliva far out, to drop it into the dust under the belly of the captain's horse. Pike's color deepened until it was tinged with purple, but he brought himself under control.

"We have no room for civilian passengers!" he snarled.

The bald-headed man shrugged. "Figured to take the stage, anyways. Guess we can still take it."

He laughed, seemingly at a private joke. But his three companions shared it.

"Shwartz," Pike barked at one of the point riders. "Go check on the other—"

"God, they were at the farm!" Mary Neat shrieked.

Every pair of eyes swung toward her. Only her head was visible, her features contorted by a mask of horror as she stared out from the front of the wagon. Cuchillo was the first man to rip his gaze away from the woman.

"It was them who helped butcher and cook—"

The civilians had only appeared to be relaxed and at ease. As Cuchillo swung his head toward them, all four were lunging into smooth, fast action. As three of them stood up, they drew revolvers from their tied-down holsters. Art reached behind him and snatched up a Henry rifle that had been leaning against the wall.

"Watch out!" the woman yelled, but the abrupt thud of boots against the stoop boarding had already warned the soldiers.

Five guns exploded.

Pike was hit twice. One bullet took him between the eyes and another smashed into his heart. He tipped sideways out of his saddle and his horse bolted. A foot was held fast in a stirrup and the dead man was dragged. Ramsey was creased across the top of his left shoulder. Shwartz had a hole bored through his stomach by a rifle bullet. Cuchillo's bullet plunged into the heart of the woodcarver.

"Inside!" the bald-headed Art yelled, plunging to the side to reach the way station's open door.

The bearded sergeant put a hand on the woman's forehead and sent her crashing back into the wagon. This meant he was too late in snatching up his rifle. As the two younger men followed Art into the building, both exploded shots toward the noncom. One bullet cut a deep furrow across his forehead. The second hit the frame of his Spencer and ricochetted into his left eye. He jerked upright on the wagon boot, spun, and plunged over the side. The second point rider was lunging out of his saddle to get behind the cover of the wagon. A rifle and a revolver shot sounded at the same time. The point rider was knocked out into the open by the sergeant's toppling body. The rifle bullet punctured his thigh and he fell with a scream. His own gun went off beneath him and exploded a bullet into his chin. From such close range the lead had enough velocity to carve a course up through the roof of his mouth and into his brain.

The revolver bullet smashed into the cylinder of Cuchillo's Colt and sent the gun spinning painfully from his hand.

Ramsey had wheeled his rearing horse and sent the animal plunging along the side of the wagon, on the far side from the way station. A fusillade of fire tracked him. One shot went low and severed a tendon in the animal's leg. The horse went down and Ramsey leapt from the tumbling mare, sliding the Spencer from the saddleboot. He landed hard but held his balance. Bullets kicked up divots of dirt around his feet. He tossed his rifle over the tailgate of the wagon and hooked his hands to climb after it. He hauled himself bodily off the ground. More gun shots sent bullets ripping through the canvas cover and thudding into the timber sides of the wagon.

Cuchillo leapt from the gelding and sprinted around the side of the way station.

"You men!" Ramsey yelled, his strident voice shattering the brittle silence that had followed the final barrage of gunfire. "There's fifty men coming up behind us."

Another silence descended around the way station and stalled wagon. Gun smoke drifted and blood ran. Then the injured horse whinnied.

"Yeah, we can hear 'em acomin'," Art snarled.

"God, where are they?" the woman groaned.

Ramsey knew the wagon with the broken tongue would not have held up the escort. But the mounted men were not coming. If they had heard the gunfire, they would have galloped into sight by now. They were a mile away, which would have been nothing if it had been only level ground. But the massive slab of rocky hillside could well have barred the sounds of the gunfight, or deflected them off in another direction.

And where the hell was the Indian? Ramsey had seen Captain Pike get it and both the point riders and the sergeant driver, too. But the last time he had seen the Apache, he was in one piece. Maybe the bastard had taken off, intent upon saving his own skin.

"Sure comin' quiet like, ain't they, Art?" one of the younger men taunted.

His words were punctuated by a barrage of revolver fire. The shots came so thick and fast Ramsey knew they were exploded from guns being fanned. But he couldn't see. There were plenty of holes in the canvas, but under the threat of the new hail of lead he had to force himself low, using his hands to press the woman hard against the floor of the wagon. Sweat beads oozed from his every pore as he recognized the possibility of a bullet exploding the boxes of ammunition loaded aboard the wagon.

The barrage ended and he raised his head and clawed at his Spencer.

"Leave it be, soldier boy!"

Art's soft-spoken words were accompanied by an abrupt brightening of light within the wagon. Ramsey spun his head, to look over his shoulder and along the length of his body. The bald-headed man was peering over the tailgate, holding the flap wide with the pointing barrel of his Henry.

Mary Neat groaned.

Ramsey unclawed his hands from around the rifle.

"On your feet and out! Both of you!"

Cuchillo Oro heard the order and watched

the officer and the woman comply—emerging from the rear of the wagon as the two younger civilians stepped out of the way station and down off the stoop. He was stretched out flat on the roof of the building, having made a half circuit, ducking into and out of the stable on the way. He had hoped to find a rifle in the boot of one of the saddled horses and discovered he had a choice of three. He selected a repeater which matched the one carried by Art. Now he waited for an opportunity to use it. He could not do so yet, for the bald-headed man continued to keep Ramsey covered.

"She ain't bad," one of the younger men said, raking arrogant eyes up and down Mary's body.

"For a breed," the second agreed.

"Strip her off," Art ordered.

The woman gasped, turned, and started to run. The two men were faster. Laughter ripping from their throats, they reached out and grasped her around the waist. One released her while the other retained his grip. A knife was drawn and inserted into the neckline of her dress. It was dragged downward.

She screamed, flailing her arms and lashing out with her legs. The two men kept up their laughter. Art maintained his gaze and the aim of the Henry at Ramsey. Cuchillo snatched a glance back along the trail to where it curved out of sight around the base of the hill. Evening shadows were advancing across the mountains. Nothing else moved out there.

"How'd she see us at the dirt farm, soldier boy?" Art asked.

He didn't have to shout. The woman's clothing had been cut and ripped from neckline to hem. The remnants of what she wore had been jerked from her to reveal her totally naked. She had ceased to struggle, suddenly aware of the futility of resistance.

Ramsey glanced at the woman, ignoring the dusky curves of firm flesh at breasts, belly, hips, and thighs. He saw only her face, contorted by horror and misery.

"I was in the barn!" she spat in reply. The man holding her had changed his grip, from her waist to her small breasts. Lust seemed to drip from his face as he kneaded the mounds, and writhed his belly against her naked buttocks. "I heard what you and the others did to those people. I smelled you cooking them."

Art spat. "Indians did the cuttin' and the boilin'. Us and the other whites just did what comes natural with the women. Show her, you guys. But save some for me."

The man holding Mary threw her to the ground. She groaned with the pain of the impact. Her captor placed a foot on her belly as he started to unfasten his pants.

"Hey, the Indian!" the other younger man snapped, whirling around and drawing his Colt.

"They had them a scout. What happened to him?"

"Got the hell out, most likely," Art growled. He showed a cruel grin to Ramsey. "Officer and a gentleman like you wouldn't like to witness what's about to—"

"Rider acomin'!"

This was from the man who had suddenly thought about Cuchillo. He pointed toward the northwest—at the far side of the hill from where the stage trail curved. Cuchillo didn't look that way. The woman did, craning her head around. So did Ramsey, the two younger men, and then the bald-headed one.

"He sure don't look like no relief column."

The sardonic comment was made by the man about to rape Mary Neat. He raked his gaze back to the woman and dropped his gun belt. His pants fell halfway down his legs. He wasn't ready for the act, and he dropped down, parting his thighs to straddle the woman's head.

"Won't be no use to you down there before you work on it up here," he taunted.

Art still had the rifle pointed at Ramsey, but Cuchillo had to risk a reflex shot by the bald-headed man. He folded up on to his knees, thudding the rifle stock against his shoulder. He squeezed the trigger and the bullet exploded blood and splinters of bones from the center of the hairless dome. Art's finger did give a dying spasm to pump off a shot. But he was already falling to the side. His bullet glanced off a wheel rim and spun into the side of one of the younger men. The man screamed and tumbled, not fatally wounded. He clawed at the ground and swung his gun.

Cuchillo's Henry made the dry sound of a firing pin failing to make contact with a shell. The uninjured man threw himself away from the head of the woman, fingers stretched to get at the holstered gun in his discarded belt. The Apache drew the golden knife.

A single gunshot exploded against the background sound of galloping hooves. It was Ramsey who fired, his bullet powering into the heart of the injured man. The would-be rapist, his pants still halfway down his legs, got his revolver clear of the holster and rolled over on to his back, looking for a target. The spinning knife made a hissing sound as it sped through the evening air. His turn had altered the target, but the new one was just as effective. The blade plunged in through his parted lips and dug into the back of his throat. His mouth closed and his lips were split by the double-edged sharpness. He sat up, then flopped back, his scream becoming a gurgle, his dying breath sending out a fine spray of blood flecked with bubbled saliva.

"Mary!" a voice roared.

Ramsey swung around, eyes and revolver covering the man who was skidding his lathered horse to a halt behind the wagon. Cuchillo merely looked, silently berating himself for not checking to see how many bullets the stolen rifle had held.

"What happened to you, gal?" Bill Neat demanded, leaping from his saddle and using the impetus to power a run toward his daughter.

But the woman was even faster. She rolled on to her belly, rose on to all fours, and lunged into the way station. She slammed the door behind her.

"Keep away from me, you bastard!" she shrieked hysterically.

Neat pulled up short, snapping his head from side to side: staring first at Ramsey and then at Cuchillo. The Apache moved to the roof of the stoop and leapt gracefully to the ground.

"What in hell's been happenin'?" he demanded.

Cuchillo ignored him. He moved across to pick up the Henry of the bald-headed man. Carefully, he ejected the shells and started to load them into his acquired rifle. Ramsey put a hand to his injured shoulder and grimaced at the crimson staining his palm.

"I want some answers, dammit!" Neat snarled.

Ramsey sagged against the wagon and turned his Colt toward the slightly built saddler. "That gives us something in common, mister," he rasped. "And you're under arrest until you can give me some good ones."

Neat, his ratty eyes filled with shock, stared around at the sprawl of bullet-shattered corpses. "I demand to see my daughter!" he yelled. "She could have been killed!"

"But she wasn't," Ramsey answered coldly.

Both men started at the sound of a shot. It had been fired by Cuchillo, to send a bullet into the brain of the wounded horse.

"And she's all right now," Ramsey continued. "She even got saved from a fate worse than death."

CHAPTER EIGHT

The rest of the wagons rolled up to the way station, the men driving and escorting them unaware of the gun battle until they saw the results of it. Lieutenant Ramsey detailed a squad to grave-digging duty, then ordered several men to offer up articles of their clothing. These were tossed into the way station, together with a blanket and a needle and some thread. As night camp preparations were made, Mary Neat was able to fashion an outfit with which to cover her nakedness.

When her modesty was protected, and Ramsey had had his flesh wound attended to, the lieutenant ordered the disarmed saddler into the station ahead of him. Two enlisted men, with shouldered rifles, stood guard on the closed door.

The mood of the men, as they ate their meal by the flickering light of the cooking fires, was ugly. But it was not Cuchillo who was the subject of their ill-humor. Ever since news had reached the train of who was missing from Fort Wylie, they had suspected Neat was responsible for the death of Lieutenant Secker. Now the rodent-faced saddler had shown up, close on the heels of more slaughter.

Lieutenant Ramsey's name was also spoken in sullen terms around the fires in the circle of wagons at the front of the way station. For the second time in a few days, he had left Wylie as a subcommander of a body of men: and had finished up as the lone surviving officer. No blame was attached to his methods. It was simply that he seemed to be a jinx. And long-time veterans of the southwestern territories were not happy to be commanded by a shavetail lieutenant from the east who had been with them for only a month.

Cuchillo took no part in the talk. He ate alone, then stretched out under a wagon, staring up at the greasy axle and willing himself to go to sleep. He was as content as he ever could be while the hated Pinner remained alive. And he now had as much as he needed to complete his mission. He had proved his worth to the horsesoldiers and he was trusted. He had a horse, a revolver, a rifle, and a job. He also had acceptance. Not friendship, as was proved by his isolation beneath the wagon while the White Eyes sat and talked in groups. One possible friend—Sergeant Duffy—was back at Wylie with a serious chest wound. Another—

the bearded sergeant—was freshly buried. No other horsesoldier—with the exception of Ramsey, whose officer ranking prevented friendship with an Indian scout—had offered him a kind word.

But this situation did not trouble the Apache. He had become a loner by the decree of fate and had grown used to it by habit. And, in the overall context of his mission to kill Pinner, he wanted it no other way. For the satisfaction he would ultimately derive from seeing Pinner dead by his hand might well be lessened if it was achieved with the aid of friendship—from White Eyes or Apaches.

He was on the very brink of sleep when the slamming of the way station door jerked him fully awake again. The talk of the men was abruptly curtailed and Cuchillo's eyes joined all others in sweeping toward the tall, slender figure of Lieutenant Ramsey.

"Sergeant!" the officer snapped at the senior noncom. "Detail four more men to guard the station. Organize a rota. Neat and his daughter are under close arrest until we reach Fort Ryan. There, as soon as a civil court is set up, they will be tried for the murder of Lieutenant Secker."

There was a burst of muttering from the men, accompanied by admiring glances directed at Ramsey as he strode into the ring of wagons and demanded a plate of beef stew.

143

"Scout!" the lieutenant yelled when he had been supplied with food.

The single word brought a renewed silence to the night camp, save for the footfalls of the four new guards as they moved to their positions around the way station. Cuchillo crawled out from under the wagon and felt every eye upon him as he approached the place where Ramsey sat. There was deep suspicion in those watching eyes, and Cuchillo had a sense of foreboding. It was obvious the men suspected the Neat father and daughter had named him. The Apache himself tried to keep an open mind, but Ramsey's hard-lined face made this difficult.

But, when Cuchillo halted, towering above the seated officer, the lieutenant's expression altered. The mouth line softened and the eyes held something akin to embarrassment. There was tacit confusion among the men.

"Injun, he knew about Pinner as well!"

The shout came from Neat, ringing out from inside the guarded way station. Now it was Cuchillo's turn to alter the set of his features. From impassiveness, his expression underwent a lightning change into deep hatred. And the looseness of his body attitude was suddenly gone. He became like a statue carved from high mountain rock: but a statue invested with volatile life, poised to spring into terrifying action.

144

"He's right," Ramsey allowed, putting aside his just started meal and holding the Apache's unblinking stare. "Colonel Zentner knew of your bitterness toward this Captain Pinner. And he told me and my fellow officers that Pinner is leading a reinforcement column to Fort Ryan."

"Who the hell's Pinner?" a man asked.

"Shuddup!" another man retorted.

"What is this to do with saddler?" Cuchillo asked, his voice as taut as his body and expression.

"Neat overheard Colonel Zentner's briefing about this column, during which your relationship with Pinner was mentioned. He knew Lieutenant Secker was responsible for assigning scout duties." Ramsey's expression hardened again. "He made a whore of his daughter. Forced her to sleep with Secker on the promise you would be assigned to this train."

"He do me favor," Cuchillo said flatly.

"Maybe," Ramsey allowed. "But Pinner's in a fort filled with soldiers. Maybe you could kill him, but you'd die in the attempt. That's all Neat cared about—your death after what you did to him at Wylie."

"Why you or Captain Pike not tell me of Pinner?" the Apache asked.

"You'd have heard," Ramsey answered shortly. "But our duty—mine alone now—is to get this train to Ryan. For that, we need a scout with his mind entirely on his job. Or maybe you would have just gone on ahead and we wouldn't have had a scout at all."

"You tell me now."

"Two reasons. I trust you, mister. I've seen you in action and I trust you. If you'd heard it from somewhere else—say Neat—maybe you wouldn't have trusted me."

Cuchillo thought about this, then gave a short nod. "What about when we get to Fort Ryan?"

Ramsey's expression became grim. "Like Colonel Zentner told us, you've done nothing against army regulations that has been officially posted. But, I'm warning you, mister, if I see you about to attack Pinner, it'll be my duty to stop you." He grinned, suddenly, as the Apache's expression tautened. "But my duty remains the same if Pinner makes the first move against you."

Again Cuchillo paused for thought before he gave a nod. "I thank you for telling me this. I can go now?"

"How far?"

"Back to wagon to sleep."

Ramsey pursed his lips. "I don't need to remind you that deserters can be shot, mister?"

Now Cuchillo showed just the trace of a smile. "Man who does not finish one job before starting another . . . that man has only himself to blame for getting in bloody mess."

The Apache received a nod of assent to his leaving, and he returned to stretch out beneath the wagon. He thought his own private thoughts, but was unable to completely ignore the voice of Lieutenant Ramsey as the officer told his men the rest of the story. The saddler had revealed the entire truth of the plot while his daughter sat in sullen silence, crouched in a corner of the way station. Now Ramsey relayed the tale to the intently listening men, filling in the details of what had happened at the fort. He told of Secker's threats about the girl, and how Neat had gone to the officers' quarters in the early hours, knocked out the man, bound and gagged him, and taken him out of Wylie through the tunnel, along with Mary and two horses.

Neat maintained he had sent Mary on ahead before torturing and killing Secker, trying to make it look like an Apache crime. He said he had given his daughter the story to tell about a long association with Secker. Everything had been done on impulse. After the barbarous murder of Secker, Neat had begun to think straight for the first time since his humiliation at the hands of Cuchillo. He started to worry about the safety of his daughter, alone in country where the Indians were turning hostile. He had tried to track her, but lost her trail. He had seen nobody until the sound of gunfire drew him to the stage line way station.

"How'd you get him to open up, Lieutenant?" a man asked.

"Held a gun to his daughter's head and told him I'd kill her if he didn't tell me what happened." The officer's voice was ice cold.

"Seems to be she could be an innocent party, sir. Would you have blasted her?"

"I don't know, soldier," Ramsey answered softly. "And neither did Neat, which was more important at the time."

A man in a group close to where Cuchillo lay made a sound of disgust. "Crazy, ain't it?" he muttered. "First he lets a guy screw his daughter just to get back at an Injun. Then he lines himself up to get hung to save her life."

"Guess he loves her in his own way," a second man answered. "More than he hates Injuns."

"He took himself an Apache squaw, for Christ sake!"

"And been tearing himself to pieces ever since, maybe."

"Sure is one mixed-up guy. I know that."

Cuchillo hovered on the edge of sleep.

"More like screwed-up."

Cuchillo slept.

CHAPTER NINE

No one had more than two hours sleep that night. The northbound stage rolled up to the station at ten with every seat taken and excess passengers riding on the roof. The sight of such a large detachment of cavalry spread relief through the tension-filled passengers, the driver, and the shotgun. The easing of fear caused them to talk fast and furiously, each one having a tale of Apache slaughter and destruction to tell.

Lieutenant Ramsey, with Cuchillo hovering close at hand, interrogated the driver of the stage, who appeared to be the most levelheaded of the civilians. At the night camp the men pumped the other newcomers with advice.

"If you're headed for Ryan, you all had better move fast, soldier," the grizzled, red-eyed driver said. "It was okay when we made our stopover. But, ever since, we been seeing more Injun signs than friggin' cactus plants, I'm tellin' you. And all of it pointin' toward Fort Ryan."

He waved an arm around the camp, indicating the groups of soldiers clustered about individual civilians. "All these folks we picked up on the way. They managed to get off their places before the Injuns hit. But we seen places after they was hit—and before the white folks could get off 'em, I'm tellin' you."

"Always Apaches?" Ramsey cut in.

"I'm tellin' you," the driver answered. "Mostly Injuns. Apache Injuns. But there's whites as well. It's a bunch of whites stirred 'em up, the rumor says. Guys runnin' guns and liquor to the Injuns. But that ain't all. Some whites is runnin' with some Injuns. And a whole bunch of drifters and gunfighters has moved into the territory. Takin' advantage of the Injun troubles to do some robbin' and killin' of their own. That's what the rumor says, anyway."

"It's not just a rumor," Ramsey answered, glancing toward the mounds of fresh-dug earth under which both soldier and hold-up man were buried.

"Maybe, maybe not," the driver went on hurriedly. "But, I'm tellin' you, soldier. Fort Ryan's where all the Injuns is headin' for. And they're headin' there fast. So, if what you got in them wagons is needed down there, you'd better get it there faster."

"Thanks for the information, mister," Ramsey said stiffly. "You can keep your advice."

He swung away from the driver and started

to yell orders at his men, to break camp, hitch the wagons and prepare to roll out.

"Ornery young shaver, ain't he?" the driver said sourly to Cuchillo.

"Troubled man never his true self," Cuchillo answered.

The driver did a doubletake at the Apache's shadowed face after hearing him talk. Then he swallowed hard. "Hey, you're an Injun."

"Apache Indian," Cuchillo supplied evenly.

The driver backed away, swallowing hard again. "Gee, the kind that's been doin' all the killin'."

Cuchillo grinned broadly in the face of the other's nervousness. "It okay," he assured. "I house trained now. Haven't scalped a White Eyes for three whole hours."

The driver did some shouting of his own, yelling across the noise of the camp breaking. "All aboard that's gettin' aboard! Further north we get, less chance of Injun trouble."

The stage rolled out almost an hour before the train moved off in the opposite direction. Bill Neat joined his daughter in the lead wagon for the final leg of the troubled journey. Both were bound hand and foot and an armed guard rode along with them. Ramsey divided his slightly depleted force between close escort and outriders. He put his continued trust of Cuchillo into action by sending the Apache far out as forward scout again.

151

The night was clear with a bright, almost full moon shining down through cold, high mountain air. There was no tracking to do, for the trail continued to be clearly defined. But, in the moonlight, Cuchillo saw many of the Indian signs the stage driver had mentioned. And he reached the same conclusions. A great many Indians were on the move, and they were all heading south.

But the gray light of a chill dawn was encroaching on the eastern dome of the sky before Cuchillo saw an Indian. It was some time since he had last made a report to the point riders and he guessed that the column of wagons was at least two miles behind him, lost to sight beyond barren ridges. And Fort Ryan, if the landmarks shown on the army chart were drawn to scale, was less than a mile ahead.

At the point from where he first saw the single Indian, the trail swooped up a long incline and then through a pass between two pinnacles of rock. Cuchillo had halted his horse at the pass, but stayed astride him, to make use of Captain Pike's binoculars. The ground sloped quite steeply away on the south side of the pass, then rose and fell like a petrified ocean —similar to the terrain where he had killed and butchered the Mohave to cheat his way into a chance at survival. But these solid waves of rock and hardpacked dirt were not smooth crested. A million years of wind and weather had tortured them into grotesque shapes. And it was at the side of such a jagged piece of natural sculpture that Cuchillo saw the Indian.

He saw a movement with his naked eye. Then, from the cover of the pass, he trained the powerful lenses on the brave. Apache for sure, with his face and naked torso daubed with war paint. Feathers in his headband. A tomahawk and knife jutting from the waistband of his hide breeches. A single shot rifle held in the crook of his arm.

The brave was a sentry, that was obvious. But wearying of the chore which he had probably had throughout the night. He continued to rake his eyes over the quarter mile of jagged hill crests to the pass, but there was a certain weary resignation about his vigilance. For many hours he had seen nothing. He was certain that he would see nothing now.

Cuchillo dismounted and stripped himself down to his leggings and moccasins. Then he tethered his horse and used the point of the golden knife to scrawl a message in the hard-packed dirt of the trail: WAIT AND KEEP WAGONS AND MEN HIDDEN SCOUT.

John Hedges had always told Cuchillo that spelling the words of the White Eyes was his weakest subject. But he could see no error as he surveyed the clearly discernible message carved into the dirt at a point where it would

153

be read before the advance guards rode through the pass.

Then he set off, carrying the Henry repeater rifle and the binoculars. But he did not move along the trail. After a full minute of surveying the terrain through the glasses, he angled out of the pass to the left. The second examination had revealed two other sentries, level with the first one and flanking him at a hundred yards to either side.

Now the entire sky was tinged with gray, paling the moon and obliterating the stars. Advancing on the left flank of the line of three braves, Cuchillo grimaced his disgust at his fellow Apaches. Not for their part in an uprising against the White Eyes. That was their affair. But he could have no respect for braves so derelict in their duties. Had he been among them, he was certain he would have spotted an intruder long before this.

However, he did not allow himself to act recklessly simply because the sentries were negligent. Night was fast going and day was marching in over the mountains. In the absence of wildlife, the silence was absolute. No matter how slovenly the sentries were, their chances of detecting the intruder were increasing with every passing moment.

But they did not detect him—until the moment before each of them died. Killing them was easier than the advance upon them, for the position of each concealed him from the others. Cuchillo circled behind the line and, until all three braves were dead, ignored the scene which was spread to the south.

Each killing was identical—in the method, the stealth, and the utter coldness. He moved in behind his victim, setting down his feet as if he had no weight at all. Then he used his weight and the strength with which it was combined. With the knife drawn ready, and the rifle and binoculars left to one side, he hooked his right arm around the throat of the sentry. The pressure of the bar of his arm cut off the startled cry. Then he jerked upward to snap the brave erect. The left hand, fisted with the golden knife, thrust forward. The blade sank into the lower back, going in up to the hilt and slicing through the kidneys. He held each man fully upright until he died, then allowed the body to fall, the weight of the corpse pulling the blade free. The spillage of blood was small.

After the third death, he turned and looked down at Fort Ryan and its surroundings. And he was thankful that the hated Pinner was down there. For the presence of his enemy justified the coldblooded killing of the trio of Apaches. If, in the future, he was troubled by bad memories, he would be able to tell his conscience that he had not murdered his brothers on behalf of the horsesoldiers: rather, because they barred his way to vengeance. But, as he alternately used the binoculars and his naked eyes, he saw that many more than the three Apaches stood between himself and Pinner. And he knew he could not kill them all.

Fort Ryan was built at the northern end of a long valley with a broad floor featured by many low mesas and rock outcrops. Here and there were deep craters which once might have been lakes. Now they held war-painted and feathered Apache braves. Other braves were hidden from the fort by the mesas and rocks. The fort itself was built on the same lines as Wylie, with a high wall along each side to give protection to the cluster of buildings inside. A major difference was that Ryan's stockade defenses and its buildings were constructed of adobe.

From his elevated vantage point, Cuchillo was able to see over the top of the gated north wall and into the fort. And it was obvious that the reinforcement column had arrived. For the sentry walkways behind the walls were solidly lined with blue-uniformed soldiers. And back-up troops, along with many civilians who had sought sanctuary from the Apache uprising, were crowded in the compound.

There was no sign that a single shot had been fired by either side and the oppressive silence continued to be clamped down upon the valley as the sky grew brighter with dawn light. At a first impression, the scene seemed to be one of stalemate. The soldiers stood with their guns cocked and ready. The Apaches sat astride their ponies; guns, bows, and lances poised for lethal use. But, for two hundred yards in all directions, the fort was surrounded by a dangerous strip of flat, coverless ground.

Cuchillo knew this would not inhibit the Apaches. They were large in number and flanked the fort on all sides. The soldiers knew the Apaches were there and knew that the Indians would make the first move. Perhaps, like Cuchillo, they knew the moment when that opening move would be made—the instant the first ray of the new day's sun shafted in over the eastern rim of the valley.

Cuchillo completed his general survey of the situation in less than fifteen seconds. He spent no more time than this seeking out two specific details of the composite whole. In the first he failed—none of the strained white faces, brought into sharp, close-up focus by the binoculars, was that of the hated Pinner. In the second, he was more successful—he pinpointed the position of the chief. He was an old warrior decked out in a feathered headdress that reached down his back to brush the flanks of his pony. He was at the foot of a mesa, surrounded by a half dozen subchiefs. Close to the top of the mesa, ready to leap aloft and signal the chief's order, was a young brave.

The old chief was staring toward the east. All other Apache eyes were directed at the top of the mesa.

Cuchillo whirled and raced back the way he had come, staying on the trail now, safe from observation and choosing speed instead of stealth. He cast frequent glances at the eastern skyline. Then he reached the pass and saw that Lieutenant Ramsey had paid heed to the message scrawled in the dirt. He sat astride his mount, at the center of a group of other riders, at the head of the stalled wagon train. Several men reached for their guns, unsure of the out-of-uniform Apache who came sprinting through the pass.

"What's the idea, mister?" Ramsey snapped, pointing at the heap of discarded clothing. "You almost got blasted."

The run had been hard and fast, but Cuchillo's breathing was regular and even. It was a sign he had recovered his full strength after the time of deprivation.

"Apaches see me in clothes of soldiers, I die first," he answered. Then he gave Ramsey a rapid résumé of what had happened since he spotted the sentries, and a report on the situation at the fort. "And attack will start when first ray of sun shines into valley," he concluded, glancing meaningfully toward the east. "Very soon now."

Ramsey thought about it for only a moment,

then nodded and looked over his shoulder along the train. "We'll make a run for it. Maybe surprise the hostiles while they're still waiting for sun up."

The word was passed back along the line of wagons. Drivers took a tighter grip on their reins. The men of the escort unbuttoned their holster flaps and cocked their rifles as they drew them from the boot. The company pennant was unfurled and raised.

"Maybe Cuchillo can stop attack," the tall, impassive-faced Apache said.

Many pairs of eyes looked at Cuchillo as they would survey a mad man.

"How, mister?" Ramsey snapped.

"Talk to chief. Make deal."

"What kind of deal?"

Cuchillo sigh. "I tell you, you say no. You must have trust you say you have."

"Don't ever trust no Injun," Bill Neat growled from inside the lead wagon.

"Shuddup!" one of his guards snarled.

Ramsey moved up into the pass without signaling for the column to follow. Cuchillo swung into the saddle of his gelding and urged the animal up alongside the Lieutenant's mount.

Ramsey was surveying the terrain with a grim expression. He heard Cuchillo move up beside him, and did not take the binoculars away from his eyes. "This deal have anything to do with Captain Pinner, mister?" he asked.

Both the officer and the scout were aware that the eastern sky was now showing a distinct tint of yellow.

"Pinner known and hated by every Apache in territory," Cuchillo answered softly. "For the life of such a man, they might spare all others."

With the three sentries dead, there was no movement to see from the pass. The ridges, where the Apache corpses lay, shielded the scene in the valley from Ramsey, who lowered the binoculars and looked at Cuchillo.

"Even if you could deliver the body of Pinner to them, I couldn't be a party to the murder of a fellow officer." There was no anger in his expression. Just regret.

The Apache nodded, completely emotionless. "And if attack comes, Pinner might die at the hand of another. You say you trust me, but Cuchillo understand what you speak. I trust you. I do not think you will shoot me in the back."

So saying, he thudded his heels into the sides of the gelding, directing the animal into a gallop along the trail. Ramsey raised a hand, but not against the departing Apache.

"Forward!" he yelled, and the line of wagons jerked into motion. But the pace was necessarily slow. Even before the lead wagon creaked through the pass, the lone Apache had ridden out of sight to gallop down into the head of the valley.

"You let him go, sir?" a corporal asked.

"I evened things up between us," Ramsey answered absently, staring at the ridge where he had last seen Cuchillo. "He saved my life back at the way station. I've just saved his."

"How's that, sir?"

"I should have shot him and didn't."

CHAPTER TEN

The hoofbeats of Cuchillo Oro's gelding provided the only sound in the big valley as he galloped the animal over the crest. But then came a burst of shouting, in both the Apache tongue and English. A nervous soldier on the wall of the fort exploded a shot, but Cuchillo was far out of range. An officer at the fort bellowed an order and the old Apache chief echoed it in his own language. The shouts of surprise died and the hoofbeats were a lone sound in the silence again.

Cuchillo stayed on the trail until he reached the bottom of the slope, then veered to the east, heading his horse toward the mesa behind which the chief waited for sunrise. Any one of more than a hundred Apaches could have killed Cuchillo with a well-aimed arrow or bullet, but the chief had called for silence, not death.

Aware he was on borrowed time, Cuchillo rode into the cover of the mesa. But he was concealed only from the soldiers at the fort.

Warpainted braves around the chief kept their weapons trained on the newcomer. The chief gave no order for the vigilance to be relaxed. His wrinkled face was impassive and his eyes were empty as he watched Cuchillo rein in his horse and dismount.

"You come unprepared for war," he accused, raking the empty eyes over Cuchillo's undaubed face and body.

"I come to wage war on one man and perhaps prevent great bloodshed," Cuchillo replied. "I am called Cuchillo Oro."

There was an excited muttering among the score or more subchiefs and braves grouped around the chief. The old man nodded, and held up a hand to silence the talk. "I have heard of the brave so named. And from your right hand I see that you are indeed he. The brave known among the horsesoldiers as Pinner's Indian."

Cuchillo listened with ill-concealed impatience. The sun was on the point of showing its leading curve above the eastern rim of the valley. "The White Eyes you speak of is in the fort."

Another nod. "This I know. You have reason to hate him more than any other Apache, Cuchillo Oro. But every brave in this valley also has hate in his heart for the man Pinner. Prepare for war, Cuchillo Oro. And, perhaps, it may be you who takes the scalp of your bitter enemy."

Cuchillo looked away from the chief, to sweep his gaze over the faces of the other Apaches gathered at the foot of the mesa. And he knew his plan was doomed to failure. Perhaps it was the White Eyes gun-runners and liquor-smugglers who had stirred up the Apaches. But they were no longer drunk and in disorganized groups. Sparks had been set off and started a fire—slow-burning at this moment, but destined to burst into white-hot anger. Pinner was the most hated man behind the walls of the fort, but there was going to be no deal for just his life. These Apaches had gathered because they hated all White Eyes. Whipped up by the effects of liquor, their hatred had become harsher when they calmed. And their determination to extract vengeance for past wrongs was as strong as Cuchillo's. All this he saw in the eyes of the Apaches grouped at the foot of the mesa.

There was a flash of white light, and the brave close to the top of the mesa vented a growl of anger. Cuchillo glanced over his shoulder, following the direction in which all other eyes looked.

The sun had not yet shafted down into the valley. But its first rays had touched the jagged ridges at the head of the valley. And Lieutenant Ramsey had made use of this. More flashes of white light stabbed out from behind the ridges

164

as the officer used a mirror to send a heliograph message to the fort.

"Horsesoldiers in hills!" the brave on the mesa called down to the suddenly suspicious chief. "They send words with light to those at fort." A pause, as the flashes from the ridges were suddenly curtailed. The brave raised himself higher to the top of the mesa and peered toward Ryan. "Those at fort use lantern to send back words!" he reported excitedly.

"Our sentries?" the chief asked. "You did not see them?"

"I saw them," Cuchillo replied. "They are in deep sleep."

"Deeper now, I think," the chief growled.

In response to the signal from the fort, Lieutenant Ramsey ordered his wagon train forward. The officer and six men burst into sight first, then the lead wagon rolled over the hill crest to spurt down the slope. Other wagons followed it in line astern, each flanked by escorts with unbooted rifles.

"Fort gates open!" the lookout atop the mesa yelled.

"I think this brave part of trick by soldiers!" one of the subchiefs snarled, his hatred for the White Eyes abruptly switched toward Cuchillo. "I think he talk with us so that more soldiers can get to fort."

The chief's eyes remained empty of expression and he showed neither agreement nor otherwise with the contention. The noise of the fast-rolling wagon train was loud and ominous in the valley. The sun showed above the valley side and shone down, hot and bright. "How say you to this, Cuchillo Oro?" the old man asked flatly.

"I say that if anyone has been cheated, it is I."

The eyes of the old man were suddenly wise. They stared at Cuchillo and the tall brave had the unnerving impression that they were looking through his skull into the workings of his brain. This could not be, he knew. But it was possible the old man was aware he had come with the soldiers. But, was he still with them in spirit?

"Then you will have opportunity to gain revenge for two injustices, Cuchillo Oro." His eyes became grim and threatening. "I will be watching you closely."

Then he glanced up at the mesa, raised his arm, and dropped it. The brave at the top snatched up a bow, ready-primed, with a flame arrow. He struck a match, ignited the oil-soaked rags, and zoomed the arrow high into the air.

Warcries were vented from every hiding place and the beat of unshod hooves added to the noise of the hurtling wagon train. Rifle fire exploded. Raised dust became tainted with the acrid taint of expended powder.

Cuchillo, aware he was under sentence of

death if he did not alter his allegiance from the army to the Apaches, swung into his saddle and joined the other Indians in galloping out from the cover of the mesa.

There were already dead and wounded, sprawled and writhing on the ground, as the group from the mesa joined the battle. Loose horses—army mounts and Apache ponies—were bolting across the valley floor, ears pricked to the gunfire and bellows, nostrils flared to the stench of powder and blood.

The plan of attack was simple, if suicidal. And the appearance of the supplies train made little difference. Groups of yelling, kill-crazed Apaches galloped their ponies toward the walls of the fort and, for long moments, Cuchillo did not understand the reason for this. Except for the north wall, where the gates were open to admit the hurtling wagon train, the defences of Ryan seemed impregnable.

But then, as he snapped off rifle shots for effect—aiming high and safe from close observation because of the billowing dust and drifting gunsmoke—he glimpsed what was happening. Many braves were blasted from their ponies, or had their mounts shot from under them. But some got through, wheeling their ponies at the last moment, as they hurled small pouches against the base of the walls. And he knew that the pouches would contain black powder. Not enough in an individual sack to more than chip the surface of the adobe. But, as each surviving attacker galloped in, tossed his sack, and swerved away, the pile mounted.

Those attacking the north wall could afford to change their tactics. And they did so. The gates would remain open for as long as a wagon remained outside the fort. Thus, while part of the force attacked the train, other Apaches galloped through a hail of lead toward the invitingly open gates.

Cuchillo was among those hitting the wagons. The tide of the battle had decreed this, and it suited his purpose. The senselessness of war forced him to kill.

He was veering in on a wagon two from the end of the column. He saw two uniformed riders through the dust. Both spotted him and it was impossible to tell if they recognized who he was. Their rifles swung toward him. Then a lance quivered through the noise-vibrating air. It thudded into the chest of one of the soldiers. Its point burst clear at his back and he was lifted, screaming, from his saddle. He died while in mid-air. Then the bloodied point of the lance was buried into the side of a wagon. The body was held suspended, swinging on the axis of the lance.

Cuchillo had to kill the second soldier himself. He put a bullet between the man's eyes as the soldier exploded a bullet which creased the Apache's upper arm. The wagon driver sent a revolver shot cracking toward Cuchillo, but the Apache was already dropping back, slowing his horse. He veered the gelding in toward the wagon with its grisly side appendage. Then he turned him hard, to race across the rear of the wagon. He kicked loose of one stirrup, and used the other foot to power a leap into the rear of the wagon.

The loose gelding crashed into a pony and an Apache was hurled to the ground. The pumping hooves of the next wagon's team pulped the body to a bloody mess. A front and rear wheel cut it into two messes. Cuchillo did not see this, for he was crawling forward. He reached the front of the swaying wagon and parted the flaps to peer out over the hunched shoulders of the driver. He could see no further than the wagon ahead, and this was merely a murky shadow in the dust.

An arrow hissed out of the dust. It thudded into the left cheek of the driver, and protruded from the right. A fine spray of blood spattered the seat. The driver stood up, his scream an unanswered plea for help. Three bullets crashed into him, and he toppled. Cuchillo reached around him to snatch the reins from his dead hands. The Apache drove from the concealment of the wagon's covering.

The rig ahead veered suddenly to the left. Instinct warned Cuchillo he should follow: that the wagon had not simply gone out of control. Two explosions crashed out, one hard on the heels of the other. Screams of agony and whoops of delight followed the double explosion. Swerving the wagon on the trail of the one ahead, Cuchillo guessed that two of the fort's walls had been breached.

The wagon he was following swerved back on to the trail again, and Cuchillo saw what had caused the deviation. The team of the lead wagon had been dropped by bullets and arrows and the rig had rolled on to its side, its heavy load of crated ammunition ripping through the canvas covering. He knew it was the first wagon for, through the billowing dust, he glimpsed two soldiers who he did not recognize, and two civilians who he did. Perhaps the guards and the Neat father and daughter had been killed by the crushing weight of ammunition crates smashing down upon them. But the attackers had not left this to chance. A tomahawk was buried in Neat's skull. A lance pinned Mary to the ground, its feathered shaft protruding obscenely from the center of her stomach. Both guards bristled with several arrows.

A third explosion temporarily drowned out all the other sounds of the battle. Black smoke rolled across in front of the hurtling wagon. Then a tongue of flame singed the hair on the backs of the team, spurring them to greater speed. Cuchillo fought for control, but within moments knew he had lost it completely. The team were in a blind panic, hurtling to inevitable destruction through the smoke and dust.

He abandoned the reins and struggled back to the tailgate of the wagon. Those which had been following were no longer there. But, through the settling dust, he saw them in the bright shafts of early morning sunlight. Both of them had suffered the same fate as the lead wagon. They lay on their sides, surviving horses in their teams struggling to escape the restraining traces. In place of the wagons, whooping braves rode their ponies in the wake of Cuchillo's rig. Several of them sent fire arrows hissing toward the crippled wagons. Canvas caught and flames licked at wagon frames and ammunition crates.

The chief was among the Apaches trailing the wagon. Cuchillo clashed eyes with the old warrior and saw friendship and trust. An order was yelled. A brave reached out to snatch at the reins of a loose pony. The brave spurred his own mount, forcing the riderless animal to match his pace. Cuchillo stepped up on to the tailgate, throwing one leg wide. The riderless pony was curved in toward him. He dropped across the animal's back and caught the reins which were hurled toward him.

A hot, powerful blast from the double explosion of both supply wagons almost hurtled Cuchillo from the back of his new mount. But he held firm with hands on the reins and knees gripped tight to the sides of the pony. And, a moment later, was the first Apache to ride into Fort Ryan through the gateway. But he was not the first Apache to get into the fort. All three other walls had been torn by explosions, and there seemed to be as many Apaches as soldiers fighting in the compound around the buildings. Certainly, Indians as well as White Eyes were toppled and crushed by the runaway team as they hauled the driverless wagon across the width of the fort.

The animals sensed the danger too late. As the far wall appeared in front of them, they tried to turn. But the impetus of the hurtling wagon was too great. Its great weight smashed the horses into the wall and spread the white adobe with a vast crimson stain.

Cuchillo skidded the pony to a halt, and fired point-blank at a White Eyes civilian who rushed toward him with a pitchfork. The man staggered backward and sat down, clutching his stomach. Cuchillo leapt to the ground and whirled. A sergeant, bleeding from a shoulder wound, charged toward the Apache, whirling an officer's saber. Cuchillo squeezed the trigger of the Henry. The rifle gave the click of an expended magazine. Then, as Cuchillo struggled to draw his revolver, the sergeant pulled up short. A tomahawk was sunk to the fullest extent of its blade in the stomach of the man.

As he toppled, Cuchillo whirled again. The chief acknowledged his responsibility with a curt nod. Then the old warrior wheeled his horse and spurred him away in search of new prey.

The tall brave hurled away the empty rifle and sprinted off in a different direction: towards the cover of a small building built close against a wall of the fort. There was just a foot or so between the rear of the building and the fort wall. As he squeezed himself into this gap, a woman screamed. Cuchillo snapped his head around, and saw her—a young white woman clutching a baby to her. Blood was coming from the unmoving lips of the baby.

"I not hurt you," Cuchillo told the woman. "My fight with one man only."

He thought the woman was mad. It seemed so from her staring eyes and the manner in which she clutched the dead child to her. But he did not trust her madness to hold her inactive against one of the reasons for her derangement. Then he saw her draw the revolver from under the baby's shawl. He could have killed her.

He chose not to.

He powered out from behind the building, feeling the draught of the bullet as it cracked past his already wounded arm. He gained the less substantial cover of a water tank, emptying its contents through a dozen bullet holes. The leakages were tainted pink with the blood of a body inside the tank.

With the Colt in his left hand and the golden knife in his right, he raked his eyes over the fort. He saw a brave's head cut clean off his shoulders by the swipe of a saber. He saw two soldiers, fighting back to back, become locked together by arrows that bored through their bodies. He saw a dying woman scalped. Then the brave who scalped her was brought down by a dozen bullets exploding pieces of his flesh away from his falling body.

There were hand-to-hand fights all over the body and rubble-littered fort. And sniping engagements between Apaches and soldiers in cover. In numerical terms of the dead and dying, no side appeared to be winning.

Then Cuchillo saw the man he had to kill. Captain Cyrus L. Pinner. It was some time since the Apache had last seen his enemy, but the White Eyes horsesoldier had not changed. In his late twenties, Pinner was a little over six feet tall and had a fine physique which weighed in the region of two hundred pounds— none of it fat. His features were basically handsome beneath a head of close-cropped black hair, but were spoiled by the perpetual sneer that adorned them.

He crouched now, in the doorway of a building on the far side of the compound from where Cuchillo watched. The doorway offered him secure cover, from which he was able to snipe with a rifle, bringing down Apaches and, on occasion, hitting the soldiers with whom the braves were grappling. Sprawled on the roof of the building was another soldier Cuchillo recognized. This was Lieutenant Ramsey, who was also sniping, but selecting his targets with greater care.

Cuchillo, his pulse racing with excitement, forced himself to remain calm as he broke from cover and began to circle the fort walls. As he rounded a heap of rubble from one of the explosions, a figure leapt down upon him. He whirled in time to see a beefy civilian, unarmed except for the two enormous hands that locked around the Apache's throat.

"Murderin' savages!" the man yelled, his face purple with rage, his hands tightening into a stranglehold.

Cuchillo forced up the Colt between their two bodies and squeezed the trigger. The man went into a spasm, but retained his hold. Cuchillo cocked the Colt and fired again. There was not even a jerk of the body this time. Cuchillo's vision blurred and his head pounded. It was just as if he was out on the desert again, long without food, water and shade. He angled the gun upward and fired the remaining bullet. The lead burrowed up through the stomach to find the heart.

"Sonofabitch!" the man snarled, and fell

backward, dead before he hit the ground. There was a massive bloodstain covering his belly. Cuchillo felt the warmth on his own belly. He did not wipe himself clean as he staggered away from the heap of rubble, discarding the empty Colt.

He was now armed only with the knife, and that was all he needed to finish what he had come to Fort Ryan to do. His throat was swollen and he had difficulty in swallowing gulps of hot, dusty air. But his vision cleared. The sun bounced off the jeweled hilt of the knife. Shots exploded and men screamed. He staggered on. Despite his resolve, he felt hot anger inside him. And he totally ignored the battle still raging around him. He could have been killed at any step of the way. But the worst that happened was that he often tripped over the slumped corpses of Apaches and soldiers.

Then he was in front of the building from which Pinner was sniping. He could no longer see the pale face of Ramsey, but he could hear the shots exploding from the roof above him. The firing from the doorway had stopped.

Cuchillo halted, and shook his head to try to clear it of the roaring sound that filled his skull. He pulled his shoulders erect and forced his stride to become purposeful. He stepped in front of the doorway, the golden knife poised for a throw.

"Look at me!" he snarled.

Pinner's repeater rifle was jammed. He was squatting down, jerking at the pump action to try to eject a spent shell case. His head snapped up and a deep hatred showed in his wide eyes. Then, as he jerked upright and started to level the rifle, fear became the dominant expression. In the moment of seeing Cuchillo, he had forgotten the rifle was jammed. But now he knew.

"Throw that knife and you're a dead man, mister!"

Cuchillo didn't have to look up at the roof above the doorway. The voice of Lieutenant Ramsey was unmistakable. The angling sunlight threw the man's shadow and that of the tilted-downward rifle across the ground.

The Apache reached a realization of his own. He had been cheated yet again in his struggle to take the life of the hated Pinner. He could have thrown the knife before Ramsey put a bullet in him. And he was prepared to die, if he could be sure that Pinner died also. But how could he be sure? The bullet would smash into him as he released the knife. And the darkness of death could descend over him before he saw the blade strike home. Cuchillo lowered his throwing arm.

Pinner's sneer contorted his features and his fear was gone. "Kill that Indian!" he yelled.

"Get out of here, mister!" Ramsey told the Apache. "I could have shot you back at the pass, but I didn't. That don't count, though. I reckon

177

this makes us even for what you did for me at the way station."

Pinner, gripped by anger now, fumbled with the jammed rifle. "I said kill him, Lieutenant!" he ordered.

"Man who stops me taking revenge, that man is my enemy," Cuchillo said softly, speaking to Ramsey, but continuing to hold his stare on the enraged and struggling Pinner.

Around the trio, the battle continued unabated. But, as if by common consent of Indians and White Eyes alike, there was no interference in the private war at the front of the building.

"After what's happened today, mister, I reckon whites and reds will always be enemies," Ramsey answered. "Now leave, or I'll do what the captain tells me."

Cuchillo looked up at the roof now, and read the determination in Ramsey's expression. He wasn't just talking. He was afraid, and he was ready to kill. "Another time," he said, and pointed his free hand into the doorway. "But I mean only him."

"Lieutenant!" Pinner screamed.

Cuchillo whirled, and set off in a loping run, heading for the hole blasted in the east wall of the fort. He remained detached from the battle, which had never been his affair in the first place.

Behind him, Captain Pinner lunged out of

the doorway as Lieutenant Ramsey dropped down from the roof.

"Shoot the frigging Indian, or I'll have you court-martialed, you bastard!" Pinner shrieked.

He pointed a trembling hand toward the running brave. But Ramsey continued to ignore the order.

"I owe him, sir," Ramsey said evenly, turned, and started to run toward the far side of the compound, where the fighting was fiercest.

Cuchillo loped toward the heap of rubble beside the hole in the wall.

Pinner vented a snarl of hatred and whirled, eyes searching for a weapon. He saw a dead Apache with a bow still clutched in his fist. He stooped, wrenched the bow from the dead hand and an arrow from the back pouch. Another raking glance showed him his running target, still in sight. He withdrew into the doorway, fitted the arrow to the bow, lined up his shot, and released the string. He vented a low grunt of triumph.

The arrow hissed across the body-littered compound to thud deep into the center of Ramsey's narrow back. The Lieutenant pitched forward, the only sound of his dying the thump of his body against the ground.

Cuchillo Oro attained the cover of a low mesa and rested, considering his situation. There had been no shots fired at him as he left the fort, for only Ramsey and Pinner were

179

aware of his escape. Every other defender of Fort Ryan was too concerned with the Apaches remaining inside the walls.

It did not take him long to reach his decision. There could be no going back. Pinner knew he was close by and would be on the alert—and would ensure that every other soldier was alerted. But still Cuchillo Oro waited at the base of the mesa, reduced to the knife, the headband, the leggings and the moccasins which had been his only possessions when he had killed and cheated his way into the trust of Lieutenant Ramsey.

Since then, there had been much more killing and cheating—to achieve what? Nothing. And this result was emphasized as the old chief led the remnants of his braves at a fast gallop out through the gates of the shattered Fort Ryan. Less than a quarter of the attacking force had survived the battle. Two more Apaches were tumbled to the hard ground as shots were triggered in the wake of the retreating braves. But then the shooting became sporadic, and faltered to a stop while the Apaches were still within range.

Like the Indians, the White Eyes had had enough of the fight. It was time for the wound-licking to begin. And time for Cuchillo Oro to go in search of a loose pony and prepare a new plan by which to slake his thirst for vengeance. But, before he turned to leave the scarred battleground, he took a final look at Fort Ryan. A figure stood in the open gateway, raking the terrain with binoculars. Like the mirror Ramsey had used to signal earlier, the lenses of the glasses were struck glancing blows by sunlight. Cuchillo no longer had binoculars to reduce the distance, but he was able to recognize the form of the hated Pinner.

"Keep looking, White Eyes!" the Apache brave rasped. "One day soon, you will see Cuchillo Oro again."

the Executioner

Order			Title	Book #	Price
_____	# 1		WAR AGAINST THE MAFIA	P401	$1.25
_____	# 2		DEATH SQUAD	P402	$1.25
_____	# 3		BATTLE MASK	P403	$1.25
_____	# 4		MIAMI MASSACRE	P404	$1.25
_____	# 5		CONTINENTAL CONTRACT	P405	$1.25
_____	# 6		ASSAULT ON SOHO	P406	$1.25
_____	# 7		NIGHTMARE IN NEW YORK	P407	$1.25
_____	# 8		CHICAGO WIPEOUT	P408	$1.25
_____	# 9		VEGAS VENDETTA	P409	$1.25
_____	#10		CARIBBEAN KILL	P410	$1.25
_____	#11		CALIFORNIA HIT	P411	$1.25
_____	#12		BOSTON BLITZ	P412	$1.25
_____	#13		WASHINGTON I.O.U.	P413	$1.25
_____	#14		SAN DIEGO SIEGE	P414	$1.25
_____	#15		PANIC IN PHILLY	P415	$1.25
_____	#16		SICILIAN SLAUGHTER	P416	$1.25
_____	#17		JERSEY GUNS	P417	$1.25
_____	#18		TEXAS STORM	P418	$1.25
_____	#19		DETROIT DEATHWATCH	P419	$1.25
_____	#20		NEW ORLEANS KNOCKOUT	P475	$1.25
_____	#21		FIREBASE SEATTLE	P499	$1.25
_____	#22		HAWAIIAN HELLGROUND	P625	$1.25

AND MORE TO COME . . .

TO ORDER

Please check the space next to the book/s you want, send this order form together with your check or money order, include the price of the book/s and 25¢ for handling and mailing, to:

PINNACLE BOOKS, INC. / P.O. Box 4347
Grand Central Station/New York, N.Y. 10017

☐ **CHECK HERE IF YOU WANT A FREE CATALOG.**

I have enclosed $_____ check_____ or money order_____ as payment in full. No C.O.D.'s.

Name_____

Address_____

City_____ State_____ Zip_____
(Please allow time for delivery.)